Streams of Mercy
in the
Valley of Shadows

Also by William F. Powers:

Children's Color Series

The New Blue Zoo (Rhyming verse) – Mr. Powers' first children's book tells a charming story about the town of Blue View which loved the color blue and built a zoo to delight all who come to visit. Available now from Amazon.com and TatePublishing.com. Includes instructions for a downloadable audio version. 32 pages, color.

The Amazing Green Flying Machine (Rhyming verse, publication schedule TBD) – The second in Mr. Powers' color series for children tells the story of an imaginative boy and his quest to build the biggest, fastest, best airplane ever and take his toy-friends on the ride of their lives. 32 pages, color.

The Pretty Purple Princess (Rhyming verse, publication schedule TBD) – The third in Mr. Powers' color series for children tells the story of a young princess who wanted everything in the kingdom to be her favorite color until the king explains to her the problems that would create. 32 pages, color.

Teens and Up

"**_Come Spring, Things Will Be Better_**" (Free short story) – A young couple deals with the anxieties of the American Civil War. While Robert is away, they write letters to keep their dreams alive and to assuage Maribeth's fears for his safety. This complete story is available as a sample of the author's work. Free PDF download at www.WilliamFPowers.com/short_stories.htm

"**_The Long Journey Home_**" (Ebook short story) – After a bitter argument with his father, an 1880s young man goes west to work on a ranch. He struggles with the potential friction when his mother falls ill and asks him to return home to see her. Available at Amazon.com, BarnesAndNoble.com, SmashWords.com, and other ebook outlets. Approx. 9,000 words.

"**_The Kindness_**" (Ebook short story) – Set in modern times, a young business consultant is falsely accused of insider deals and must fight to uncover the truth and restore his good name. Available at Amazon.com, BarnesAndNoble.com, SmashWords.com, and other ebook outlets. Approx. 8,500 words.

"**_Riverboats and Roses_**" (Ebook short story) – A riverboat captain has been killed in an accident leaving his family to grieve his passing. But the widow struggles with memories of an argument for which she can no longer ask forgiveness. Available at Amazon.com, BarnesAndNoble.com, SmashWords.com, and other ebook outlets. Approx. 6,000 words.

Visit www.WilliamFPowers.com for updates and other titles.

Streams of Mercy
in the
Valley of Shadows

~~~

A soldier finds redemption
on the other side of broken.

~~~

William F. Powers

Printed by CreateSpace
ISBN-13: 978-1492779001

This book is a work of fiction. Except for the Vietnam War in general and the mentions of Hong Kong; Schenectady, NY; the state of Oregon; the Grand Canyon and the two sporting events referenced herein, the characters and places and events are products of the author's imagination. Any resemblance to persons, living or dead, or places or events is coincidental and unintentional.

Bible quotations are from The King James Version (KJV), Oxford University Press.

~~~

Reader comments

"This is very realistic." ~ Jerry M., Vietnam Veteran

"This is so good. Just keep the books coming." ~ Nancy A.

"A good story and a great message. I saw myself in there in quite a few places as I'm sure a lot of people will when they read it." ~ Harold L., Veteran

Dedication

This book is dedicated to all the men and women in uniform—past, present, and future—the protectors of our freedoms. Because of your sacrifice, your fellow citizens are safer and the world is a better place. Thank you for your service to our country.

There isn't enough room to individually list all those to whom I dedicate this book. That said, please allow me to specifically mention the following veterans: Ralph Gibbs, Harold Leist, Ken Marguet, Bill Mueller, Jerry Morgenroth, Jef O'Connell, Wayne Schlichter, Joe Thompson, Ron Zigelmier, and my father, Max H. Powers.

Inscribed on a rock at the Vietnam War Memorial in Odessa, Texas are the words, "Not everyone who lost his life in Vietnam died there. Not everyone who came home ever left there." I was a young man during the days of American involvement in Vietnam. Though I was never asked to serve there, I identify with those who did. They are my generation, I think of them as my people, and I especially dedicate this book to them.

~~~

O beautiful for heroes proved in liberating strife.
  Who more than self their country loved and mercy more than life!
    America! America! May God thy gold refine
      Till all success be nobleness and every gain divine!

Katharine L. Bates

Streams of Mercy
in the
Valley of Shadows

Forward

Disagreements about the need, wisdom, and propriety of any specific military conflict are older than our country itself. These are debates in which any free people must engage, hopefully without rancor and ill will.

This story will not end those arguments; it is not intended to. Instead it creates a word-picture of the very real struggles of one person in one war, the effect it has on his life, and the impact he has on the lives of others.

However, one need not be in a war to endure strife. Conflict occurs on foreign soil, but just as surely, it also happens in the recesses of the human soul. The bruises, cuts, and wounds are real regardless of the source, and they are painful.

The good news is that there is hope, there is redemption, and there is healing. I hope, as you read, you will find all three.

William F. Powers
Southwestern Ohio
September, 2013

Part 1

Chapter 1 – The Nightmare

On a scale of one to ten this was at least a fifty. Sgt. Tom Jenkins was not sure how long it had taken, but it felt like eternity since the ambush started. It seemed like the whole war had just taken place in front of his eyes. Of all the nightmares Tom had experienced during his time in Vietnam, this one was by far the worst.

At any fraction of a second, there were dozens of bullets in the air, and it was just a continuous barrage. Pieces of pointed lead headed one way at twice the speed of sound and just as much traffic headed back the other way.

Explosions interrupted the continuous sounds of bullets hitting trees and rocks. There were also the repeated ticks and cracks as bullets ripped through leaves and twigs on their way to the next solid object. Every living thing at both ends of the fight was hoping *it* was not the next solid object.

They had been on a routine patrol when they were ambushed. Tom only stopped firing because his magazine was empty, but in that moment of personal silence, he realized that the sounds of gunfire and grenades had ceased. There were still noises off in the distance. Birds squawked as they continued their escape from the startling racket; the underbrush rustled as creatures scurried away, unconvinced that the noise had ended for good.

Tom was not convinced either. As he listened to the relative calm, he removed his empty magazine and installed a full one. He knew he should work quietly so the enemy would not be aware of his location. At the same time, the ambush had angered him, and he was tempted to bang the magazine into place as if to announce loudly that he was reloading and ready for round two.

In reality, he hoped there was no round two. But there was. Almost as soon as his fresh magazine snapped into place, the air was filled with lead again. Tom returned fire, and the battle raged on.

Before the brief silence, he had seen two of the squad, including the radioman, take hits. Now out to his right, the squad leader Lieutenant McDonnell went down. He looked over to his left just as "Moon-shot" dropped his M16 and crumpled to the ground.

The fighting continued for another eternity.

The Vietcong had surprised them, and the team didn't have time to position themselves for an effective defense much less any counterattack. The VC had pinned them down and were taking full advantage of their upper hand.

There was a machine gun nest about two hundred feet up the path and a small village, a dozen huts on a small rise, just beyond the nest. The machine gun was responsible for much of the carnage inflicted on the team; the rest of the fire was coming from up in the shanties. Gunfire from both sources had seriously decimated the squad.

Tom had one grenade left. He crawled over and took two from Moon-shot who was covered in blood from a neck wound. "Hang in there, Moon; we're gonna get you out of this," he told him. Moon-shot gave a small grin of approval but then grimaced in pain as he coughed. Tom placed a cloth on his neck and told him to press it as firmly as he could.

Hand grenades were often lobbed short distances from behind a bunker; however, if he was going to keep his promise to Moon-shot, he was going to have to call on the skills he had developed as the center fielder for the Johnstown High School Tigers. He figured that to create as much chaos as possible, he needed two grenades to go off together as close to each other as possible and preferably right in the middle of that nest.

Larry Pullman was the only one Tom could see still manning a position. "Larry," he shouted over the noise. "Larry!" When Larry looked around, Tom showed him the two grenades and motioned his plans. Larry nodded in understanding, motioning back that he knew what to do.

Tom put a full magazine in his M16 and pulled the pins on both grenades. He motioned a countdown to Larry, and then on "one", he simultaneously threw one grenade high like a pop-up and released the safety lever on the other. Then in a quick motion, he threw the second one as if he were throwing out a runner stealing home. He had not lost his touch. Almost in the same instant, the pop-up landed right in the nest while the second one landed just short and bounced in. As VC started scattering, Larry began shooting.

Tom grabbed the third grenade and his rifle. Once his two hand deliveries had taken their toll, he began to run toward what was left of the nest adding his gunfire to Larry's. As he advanced, he threw the third grenade as far as he could up toward the shanties on the rise. The third explosion, added to the realization that their first line of defense had been knocked out, sent the VC in the tiny village scrambling out the far end.

Tom was out of grenades and low on rounds when the firing tapered off to occasional reports. By now, he was taking his shots very carefully. Out of the corner of his eye, he saw a shadow move in the doorway of a hut. The motion was followed by a glint off some shiny object. Tom placed a single shot into the darkness inside. There was a shriek and a clamor; then all motion stopped.

Several more shots rang out from the far end of the village followed by some commotion beyond the village that faded into silence.

Larry had been hit in his left shoulder during the final skirmish but was able to cover Tom while he cautiously retreated to where the team originally had been pinned down. Then Larry stood guard while Tom began to size up the situation. He checked Lieutenant McDonnell; he was dead. Tom began to call roll softly but got no replies. He went over to check Jerry, the radioman; he was dead too. Tom took the radio with him as he cautiously moved from one man to another, occasionally glancing up the hill from where the ambush had emanated. He found that he alone had escaped unharmed. Moon-shot was now unconscious from his neck wound, and Larry was the only other man still alive.

Tom radioed for evacuation choppers and then told Larry to start moving Moon-shot and the others to the clearing where the choppers would land.

Normally he would have moved to the evac location with Larry and set up a defense perimeter but something didn't seem right. He carefully crept toward the village. A number of VC lay scattered on the ground. He checked each carefully before he went on to the next, constantly scanning the surroundings for motion or anything else that might suggest danger. As he approached the hut from which the shadowy motion had come, he could hear muffled sounds. He hesitated for a moment. With a careful eye on the hut, he checked the other victims of the action that Larry and he had unleashed. When he finally reached the hut, he peered in and found a frightened, sobbing little girl standing over an elderly woman who lay on the dirt floor. Tom's shot had found its mark in her chest.

The little girl was probably eight or nine years old; the old woman was easily eighty, maybe older. They both wore tattered clothes, and the girl had no shoes. Cautiously, he went into the hut causing the youngster's crying to increase in both volume and alarm. The woman was unconscious, but the child was painfully aware of everything. As Tom drew closer, she stood her ground, instinctively becoming a guardian for the one who had evidently been guardian to her until mere moments before. Her face was filled with panic but simultaneously steeled with determination.

The little one protested as Tom checked the old woman's wound. He decided she might survive.

He heard the Hueys in the distance and picked up the woman as the child pulled on her arm and screamed something in protest. "Giúp!" Tom yelled, using the only Vietnamese word he knew for giving help. Then he repeated more softly, "Giúp. Giúp". The child eyed Tom suspiciously and continued to hold onto the woman but no longer pulled against him. Tom carried the woman out of the hut and down the hill toward the clearing; the child followed closely holding tightly to the old woman's dress.

~~~

They collected the rest of the bodies and got them onboard the choppers. The flight back to base seemed a lot longer than it actually was.

The frightened look on the little girl's face spoke volumes. There was fear of being in this huge, loud, metal machine; fear of what was to become of her; and fear for the old woman who was probably a grandmother or even a great grandmother. The girl had no idea that she was sitting next to the very man who had shot her friend. She had no way of knowing that he had mistaken the old woman for a combatant.

For the first time during his tour, Tom found himself questioning one of his decisions. The intolerable noise of the chopper faded into the background of his mind as he agonized over his shot. The old woman might die, and he could have hit the little girl just as easily. Where were her parents? Was anyone left in the village? Had the VC run them out? Or killed them?

His thoughts drifted far away to Johnstown. Marsha was there; she was safe. He was glad for that but wished he were there as well. He had not spent much time thinking about her amidst all the fighting and other war zone activities. When he left for Vietnam, they were not as close as they had been when they married the year before. She wrote him letters, but he was not good at writing back. Even when he did write, it was short and usually on the more trivial and mundane aspects of his experience—the weather, some routine patrol he had been on, a poker game, or the food. He never had been good at expressing his feelings, and being in Vietnam had not changed that. Nevertheless, he missed being home—and he missed *her*. He promised himself to write her a letter after he made his report. He had made many such promises after skirmishes, but he usually forgot after the emotions died down. This promise was forgotten also, at least for now.

~~~

The report was hard to fill out. Moon-shot had died just as the choppers arrived, so everyone except Tom and Larry left their lives just outside that little village. His mind flashed back to another battlefield in a different time. The president's words rang in his ears, "the last, full measure of devotion".

Tom mentioned the old woman in his write-up, but he did not mention how she was wounded. Normally Lieutenant McDonnell would have filled out the report, but Tom was the ranking survivor so the duty fell to him.

When Tom turned in the report, Captain Upton skimmed through it. "Good job out there, Jenkins," he said. "It is tragic to lose so many good men, but you stepped up to the plate. I saw Pullman in medical, and he told me what you did. I want you to know that I will be putting you in for a Commendation Medal." Tom was not sure what to say; he just did what he needed to do.

"Thank you, sir." Then after a pause, he inquired, "Permission to be dismissed, sir? I want to check on Pullman."

"Sure. I think he will be fine, but I imagine you guys have a lot to talk about."

The two exchanged salutes, and Tom left. Moments later, the captain heard someone retching outside his window.

~~~

Tom went to medical where a nurse assured him that Larry's injury was not serious. The doctors were busy with wounded from another battle further north, but they would take care of Larry as soon as they could. The two young survivors talked for several minutes. Eventually, the nurse came in. "One of the doctors is free now; I need to take you back, corporal."

Tom walked out, sat on the ground outside medical, and leaned back against the structure. His mind played back the events of the day like a bad movie. The toll of the last several hours was starting to dawn on him. Tom had never found it easy to develop close friendships; he only had one really close buddy in high school. However, life and death environments develop strong trusts and deep bonds. These guys were his family here, and only he and Larry had survived this latest scene in "The Nightmare".

As he sat there, he heard crying. It was not a man but not a woman either. It was the crying of a child. He looked toward the mournful wail. Twenty or thirty yards away, he saw a nurse trying to comfort the little girl from the village. Tom could not hear the nurse; it didn't make any difference because he did not know much Vietnamese. He could only guess what the nurse was saying, but whatever it was, her words had set that precious little soul adrift on a sea of grief. Though he did not understand the words, he *could* understand the anguish in every sound that poured out of that sobbing, pain-distorted, little mouth.

"You and me too, little girl," he sighed softly. "You and me too." He had caused her pain, someone else had caused his pain, and in the tomorrows to come the story would repeat again and again.

Tom wiped his eyes, stood up, and headed back to his barracks.

~~~

"WHAAA ... ?!" was the only sound that came out of Tom's mouth, but it was accompanied by the squeaks that shriek from a bunk when a sleeping body flashes into an upright position. It was as if a spring-loaded lever was released, only to stop suddenly at the end of its travel. His heart was beating faster and harder than a rip from a machine gun, and his breathing was trying to keep up. Every muscle was strained, ready for his next move ... whatever he decided that needed to be.

After a moment, he realized he was not back at the village as he had dreamed but instead was sitting on the edge of his bunk wearing a tee shirt he was sure contained at least a gallon of sweat. He had lost seven pounds in the three weeks since the attack.

This startled awakening was not Tom's first. It had happened several times just after his arrival in 'Nam, but after a week or two, his nerves settled down. Now, with the exception of one night last week, it had happened every night since the village incident, usually more than once in the same night.

His arrival in this war-torn jungle had begun a completely different period in his life, but the village ambush was a dividing point; it put that altered life on steroids. Everything became louder, closer ... more personal. Some guys didn't have this trouble, or if they did, Tom couldn't see it. He was sure no one would understand, so he just kept quiet, biding his time. There was only one thing he was sure of: "I am *not* going to re-up to come back here!" he muttered under his breath. His breathing was just now starting to come back into the normal range. He added a few more choice words to the end of his vow, some becoming louder than he had intended.

Someone across the room stirred, turned over, and went back to sleep.

Simply put, Tom's rest wasn't any rest at all. He was not a morning person anyway, but this constant interruption to his sleep made the sunrise more unwelcome than it ever was. He thought his apprehensions hadn't affected his work or his attitude so far; he was pretty sure that he had been able to guard against that.

~~~

"Jenkins, what's the matter?" Almost five weeks had passed since the village conflict. Tom had been summoned to Captain Upton's quarters. There was not as much condemnation in the question as there was recognition of a potential problem with a goal to minimize the impact on the rest of the troops—and on Tom himself.

"Nothing, Captain," Tom replied. "It's just this war."

"Don't let it get you down, Soldier. We're here to do a job, and we need to stay focused on the mission as long as we're in the zone. Otherwise, somebody gets hurt."

"Yes sir" is what came out of Tom's mouth, but what was going through his mind was a lot different. It had been more than a month since the ambush, but Tom was still struggling with the unbelievable event. The death of so many of his buddies, the shooting and subsequent death of the old woman, the anguish of the little girl ... it all bothered him deeply, but he found that he couldn't open up about it to anyone except on a surface level. Additionally, it caused him to second-guess himself; he was slower in making decisions when making the right choice quickly was crucial. He was less sure of himself and feistier with others. He thought he was hiding his uncertainties from everyone, but he was the only one who thought that.

The captain dismissed him. Tom snapped a salute and turned to leave. After a few steps, he paused a moment, then turned back.

"Sir?"

"Yes."

"I think it would be a good time to take my R&R," he said. Personnel got one extended 'Rest and Relaxation' per tour in 'Nam; Tom thought that it might help him forget things and get back on top of his game.

"Good idea. Fill out the request, and we'll get it in for you."

"Thank you, sir."

"You bet."

They exchanged salutes again, and Tom left.

"The Nightmare" was Tom's description for the war since shortly after he arrived. "Nightmare is the word!" he thought to himself. The idea of seeing another part of the world had intrigued him at first, but after just a week or so in 'Nam, he decided that this was not what he had in mind. He wasn't sure the war was right but wasn't sure it was wrong either. Regardless, these poor people sure were mixed up in a mess, and what a mess it was! Some were fighting against their own countrymen while others weren't fighting at all but still suffered from the conflict that surrounded them.

Tom put in his request for Hong Kong. He had heard a lot from the guys who had been there and decided that would be a good place to shake this monkey off his back.

He finally wrote the letter to his wife. Marsha's letters were among the few he got from home, and though they had been getting on each other's nerves by the time he shipped out, the separation seemed to smooth things over a little. He enjoyed reading her letters as a connection with home, but he was not good at returning the favor and rarely wrote enough that it would get crowded on a postcard.

"Dear Marsha, This place is a mess, and I can't wait until I get out of here. I saw Glenn Abney a couple weeks ago. His unit borrowed one of our generators, and he drove the truck that came to pick it up. I am leaving for R&R soon. Tom."

Tom did not mention the village incident. He might have been able to talk it over with Glenn, but the generator pickup occurred several days before the ambush. They hadn't seen each other since.

Tom met Glenn during their junior year at Johnstown High School, and they become like brothers. The village incident was one thing that he would not share with anyone else; he wasn't sure he could even share that with Glenn.

Glenn had been born and raised on a small farm in the Texas Panhandle near Memphis, and his heritage included a strong telltale accent. The June before his junior year, Glenn's sister Elizabeth had moved to Oregon with her husband and daughter. Three weeks later, their father had his heart attack. After their dad died, Glenn's mom sold the farm, and she and Glenn moved to Johnstown to be near her mother. Glenn was laidback with a relaxed nature. Although his dad was gone and his mom had passed away shortly after his arrival in Vietnam, he maintained a relatively happy disposition.

On the other hand, Tom had a more fiery personality. He was abandoned at an orphanage when he was two months old and placed in several foster homes. When he was five, his life took a turn for the better when a kindly couple adopted him and he became the only child in their home. Tom's anger began to resurface when his adoptive father was killed in a boating accident several weeks before Tom turned sixteen. Things only got worse when his mother was diagnosed with cancer and died the summer after he graduated from high school.

Both Tom and Glenn were introverts. Neither of them felt comfortable in social settings, but they developed a close bond with each other. Tom liked to work on cars; Glenn had worked on the tractors and equipment around his dad's farm. After school, they could often be found together near one machine or another surrounded by tools and greasy parts.

~~~

More weeks passed … more of the same.

Then, "FINALLY, FINALLY, FINALLY!" Tom thought. He had received his R&R orders, been on two flights, and sat through the do-and-don't lecture at the R&R Center. "Free," he thought to himself. "I am free from that rat-hole nightmare, even if it is only for a couple days. This is going to make me a whole new man."

The bus dropped him off at the hotel, and he had hardly checked in before Tom found a bar and had a beer in his hand. Then it was only another couple of minutes before he was working on his second. He was going to do whatever it took to forget the months he had spent in The Nightmare and to numb himself to the realities of that world. And he didn't have a minute to lose!

After four beers, maybe five—he lost count—Tom started to loosen up. He recognized several other guys who had come over on his plane. After they chugged down a couple drinks, they began to gravitate toward some of the women in the bar. Tom started eying the ladies too. He knew that he should not start down that road, but by then, his blood alcohol level wasn't helping his decision making process. The little voice in the back of his mind told him that nobody would ever know. The problem was that the voice failed to mention that *Tom* was somebody and that *he* would know. Knowing better or not, his impetuous self not only went down that road, he followed that road all the way back to his hotel room.

~~~

She was a pretty, Vietnamese woman in her early twenties who fled to Hong Kong last year after her parents and brother were killed in a village attack. Linh had hired herself out to be Tom's guide and companion during his stay which was a practice of some of the young women in several of the cities approved for R&R.

Tom awoke as morning light began to fill the room. She had gotten dressed and was sitting on the floor against the wall.

"What's your name again?" he asked, holding his head in an attempt to control the pounding.

"Trung Linh. It is meaning 'spirit of gentleness'," she told him, standing up.

"Trong Lin?" Tom tried to imitate.

"Yes. You like?"

He motioned to her with the bottle he had brought with him from the bar last night. "It's a beautiful name," he grinned with one eye half closed. He took another swallow, but the beer was warm and flat. "It's a beautiful name," he repeated.

There was more beer talking than kindness or respect, but Linh seemed pleased with his answer. She smiled and bowed gently. "You like to see city now?" she asked wide-eyed, smiling and nodding her head with enough energy that her coal black ponytail bounced out from behind her head.

"Yeah," he said. "Yeah, but I'm going to clean up first. I'll be out in a few minutes." He took his clothes into the bathroom and closed the door behind him.

~~~

Linh knew Hong Kong well and showed Tom many of the sights and stores. He purchased a rather expensive camera, a significant change from the Eastman Kodak Brownie his mom and dad had given him for his thirteenth birthday. He also bought a telephoto lens, a camera case, and twelve rolls of film. He asked the shopkeeper questions until he felt comfortable with his new purchase, and soon he was taking pictures of the sites as Linh guided him around the city.

Tom had not had breakfast; hangovers made him lose his appetite for anything except another beer. He did have some coffee as Linh ate breakfast, but a little before noon, he began to get hungry.

"Where's a good place to eat?" he asked.

"I know good place about three block," she replied. "Come. You see."

After two blocks, they turned onto Baker Street. He thought it was an odd name for a street in Hong Kong. He later noticed that several other streets in the area had English names and attributed it to British influence.

The restaurant was not even on the main street. As they walked along Baker Street, she turned down an alley and they went to the far end. There they entered a single door in the side of the building. It took a few seconds for his eyes to adjust to the dim lighting, but he could tell by the aroma that he was in a place that served good food. He didn't really like spicy hot food, but he did like it to have a lot of flavor. The aroma told him that the food here probably had more flavor in a single bowl than his mess hall served in an entire month.

They sat at a table, and a small older woman came over and spoke to Linh. Tom didn't know what they were saying, and it looked like they were having a little trouble communicating, but he could tell that they knew each other. They spoke briefly, and then Linh turned to him. "What you like?" she asked.

"Chicken or beef with vegetables and rice," he said. "But not hot," he added quickly.

Linh placed the order and then turned back to Tom. "Do you know her?" he asked. "Is she a friend?"

"No, not friend. I know her from come here."

"Do you eat here often?"

"Maybe two, three time in the month. When I am—how you say—in the place?"

"When you are in the area?" Tom asked.

"Yes, that is the words." She lowered her head and looked up grinning sheepishly, a little embarrassed that she had not remembered the phrase.

Tom smiled back at her. She was a pretty girl. She was also pleasant. They had been together almost sixteen hours and had not exchanged one angry word. He didn't remember the last time he could say that about him and Marsha. They had several arguments on their honeymoon, and as their first year unfolded, heated words became more and more common. Tom knew that he was probably the cause of some of their strife. Marsha told him regularly that it was *all* his fault; each time she did, it just started another fight.

Tom also realized that Linh was working for him, so being nice was probably just part of the job. But it seemed like more than that; she seemed like a really kind person.

They laughed and talked as they ate their lunch. They both had been right: this was a "good place", and the food was very flavorful.

~~~

He wasn't sure when it happened but somewhere between "It's a beautiful name" and the time they left the restaurant, Tom stopped thinking of Linh as a business arrangement and began to enjoy her as a friend. He insisted that she pose for a picture in front of the Wong Tai Sin Temple and again at Victoria Harbour. Before long, Tom was including her in many of his shots and would often ask someone to take their picture as they posed together.

Over the next several days, they visited a number of historical sites; she knew a little history about most of them. They took the Star Ferry between Victoria Harbour and Hong Kong Island each day and went to Victoria Park twice. Both the park and the harbor had been named for the nineteenth century British monarch, another sign of The Crown's impact on the culture.

The time for Tom was the dream of a lifetime—a peaceful, refreshing, personal island. That island was right in the middle of a raging sea of war, a war which was just one more unsettled place in the larger setting of Tom's angry life. Like a child playing in a warm summer rain, he was completely immersed in the sensations of the moment. Nothing else mattered.

~~~

On the flight back to 'Nam, Tom's anticipation level was a lot lower than it had been on the trip to Hong Kong several days earlier. Tom stared out at the smears of white that streamed past the window as the plane climbed into the clouds.

Actually, he was in a better frame of mind. Well, sort of. The change had distracted him from the frustrations and anxieties of the last months. But now, his life had new complexities. He had developed an attachment to Linh and had the impression that she liked him in return. He had even considered going AWOL and asking her to go to Ceylon with him. He could have gotten a job as a mechanic; no one would have thought to look for him there. He never got up the nerve to ask her.

When they last parted company, he watched her walk out of his life and back into the bar where they had first met. They had spent every last possible moment together. If he had gone back in after her and she rejected him, he would have been late. Not wanting to go AWOL without Linh, he just abandoned the idea, left his hope behind, and headed back to the R&R Center.

The more Tom thought about it now, the more regrets he had. His mind went through a cyclone of possibilities and what-ifs until the frustration, anger, and guilt begin to surface again. After several minutes, he realized what was happening to his emotions and decided to let it go, for the sake of his own sanity. That reduced the anger and frustration somewhat but not the guilt—neither about the old woman nor about Linh.

~~~

The next several months were increasingly tense for Tom. He went out on patrols regularly with his new unit, but there were things that continued to attract the attention of his superiors. Tom's moods, talk, and general demeanor suggested he was not doing as well as he had even before his R&R.

Once again, the captain called him in for a talk.

"Jenkins?"

"Yes, sir."

"You seem to be sitting on a beehive, Jenkins."

"A beehive, sir?"

"Yes. You're snapping at the guys, getting into tussles. Listen, a little in-your-face with another branch of service in a bar back in the

States is one thing. But you are causing grief with your own guys in a war zone. That disrupts unity, Soldier, and that is not a good thing!"

"Yes, sir. I mean no, sir."

"Now, what's this all about?"

Tom had not noticed that his emotional baggage was showing again. He couldn't tell Captain Upton what had happened with the village woman. It truly was an accident, but he had not been completely forthcoming in his report. He had even gotten the medal. Although it had nothing to do with the old woman, it was for the same incident. It would just make things messy. And the thing with Trung Linh, well, that could lead to other problems. He would never even mention that to Glenn; he was a back-home friend, and Tom didn't want that incident to accidentally spill out in front of Marsha.

"Just the war, sir. I am getting short, and I guess ..."

"I understand, Soldier," the captain interrupted, raising his voice, "but I have to keep my command focused on the business at hand, or we start making mistakes. That is unacceptable!"

"Understood, sir."

Tom was down to his last few weeks and he had been a good asset to the platoon so Upton was hesitant to really come down any harder on Tom. At the same time, internal strife was a negative he could not allow to fester under his command. "You need to buck up, Jenkins, or your next tussle is going to be with me. And trust me, Soldier, you do not want that."

"No, sir!"

After dismissal and salutes, Tom headed back to his quarters. He just had to keep this thing together! Now that the end was within sight, the last thing he wanted was to get tangled up in some disciplinary action that interfered with his return to civilian life.

~~~

It was an unusually gorgeous morning. Tom was not sure how much of it was weather and how much of it was the fact that in a few hours he would be heading out on a quest that would include a plane headed east. His trip was about to start and wouldn't end until he was one-third of the way around the world. Tom would prefer to be even farther from this place but would settle for eight thousand miles or so.

"I made it," he thought. "I made it without even a scratch!" He was right about his body, but he was not thinking about the scars that had collected in his mind and on his heart.

He had packed most of his belongings last night and was eager to get underway. Breakfast, clean up, some final packing...then he would board the bus and begin his journey home.

~~~

The plane slowly bumped its way along the tarmac and then executed its turn onto the runway. The engines roared into a noisy demonstration of power. After a few moments, the brakes released, and the huge metal machine started rolling down the long concrete lane. A satisfied smile came over Tom's face as the plane lifted off; the next leg of his long-awaited return home had begun.

Home. That sounded so good to him! Maybe Marsha and he could get back on track. They had really gotten off into the emotional weeds; perhaps this time apart had helped to smooth things out. Yeah, things were going to be better. Finally.

Last night had been filled with the anticipation of this moment. It had not afforded him much sleep. Thoughts of leaving Vietnam, of being home, and of a better marriage became an emotional trifecta that melted into the gentle bounce of the plane as it climbed into the clouds. Before long, his thoughts became his dreams.

~~~

Turbulence bumped Tom out of his slumber. He looked at his watch and realized they should be near Hong Kong about now. His warm thoughts suddenly had an intruder; it was another warm thought but one which conflicted with the others. He tried to go back to sleep, but sleep was not the familiar friend that it had been just an hour before.

Chapter 2 – Homecoming

Tom's enlistment was complete. They tried to get him to re-up, but he wasn't having any part of it. He had seen all he needed to see to make *that* decision. Army life in general and Vietnam in particular had disabused him of any romantic billboard promises. There wasn't a big enough carrot in the world that they could dangle in front of him to change his mind. Period.

Some of the returning personnel had a good sense of their purpose in the war effort. They heard about the things people said about them back in the states. However, except for a few bad apples, they knew they had conducted themselves professionally and honorably notwithstanding the fact that they were in a war.

For Tom, the time had come. He found himself sitting at a table, signing papers and being processed out. "Not soon enough," he thought as he signed. His mind wandered off to the tasks before him; he had phone calls to make and a one-way bus ticket to buy.

~~~

His arrival back in Johnstown was a very happy one. Marsha and he were friends again. She chided him about not writing more, and more often, but all seemed to be right with them and with the world.

Tom and Marsha had rented a little bungalow just before he was drafted. For several weeks, there were visitors dropping by, inviting them over for dinner, or scheduling a night out. Once old friendships were renewed, the activities slowed down to a normal pace.

Tom talked to the service station manager where he had worked before he was drafted, but he didn't have any openings. After several weeks, he found a machine operator's position at Morgan Manufacturing, a fabrication company several miles from the house. Things were good again.

Occasionally, Marsha expressed concerns over Tom's drinking with his buddies, but he didn't think it was a big deal. "I can handle it," he assured her. Besides, she liked her nights out with the girls, and he was just having some fun with his friends. However, when a

Friday night bar fight earned Tom a sleepover in a jail cell, Marsha was furious. She insisted that he get some help. He promised that he would settle down and that seemed to bring things back into balance. It would become a tense balance.

A tree branch is actually strengthened by being swayed in the wind, and it can even be bent severely by a gale or a passing animal without injury. But when the pressure is great enough, cracking sounds give warning that serious damage is imminent. By the time the cracking starts, even though the branch could heal, there is a permanent change to the tree, be it ever so slight.

Things in their home were starting to emit cracking sounds. Tom's tense balance was somewhat less assuring to Marsha. Over the next few months, Tom continued his drinking with his friends. There were no more altercations, at least none that ended up with police intervention, but Tom's temper became more of an issue. In the interest of maintaining some level of peace at home, Tom did not make Marsha the target of his anger; however, she would see his temper flare at perceived injustices in conversations or on TV, particularly when the subject was the war or draft dodgers. War protesters were right up there at the top of his list of hot buttons.

Things continued to cool with Marsha and that added to Tom's frustration. The good-to-be-home sensation which had floated him during his first month back had faded to a good-to-be-with-my-buddies feeling, but that wasn't what he had envisioned on the long flight back from The Nightmare. He had assumed that spending hours in a fast-moving airplane would separate him from the memories he was trying to leave there, but memories don't live in a country, they live in a mind. He had brought that back with him.

~~~

Marsha left on Sunday to go with her Aunt Renee on a dulcimer concert tour. Aunt Renee had played the instrument since she was in her teens and was really quite good. The Johnstown Dulcimer Club met in the basement at the First Presbyterian Church and had an outstanding reputation for their local performances. They were all excited when Mrs. Lancaster announced that she had finalized details for the four-concert tour she had mentioned during their previous practice. Since Uncle Martin didn't like to travel, Aunt Renee asked Marsha to go along with her.

Tom was alone for the week. Marsha and he had fallen back into arguing, so he was glad for the break. He had been at work all day and stopped to do a little fishing on the way home. While backing up, he accidentally scraped the truck against a tree down by the river. The truck was old, but it was his. It angered him that now the warped door made a scraping noise when he opened it.

He got home about the time the game was to start. This was the first time a World Series game would be played at night, and Tom was looking forward to watching it. He had watched Saturday's game. On Sunday, the game was rained out, so he had to listen to the makeup game and game three on the radio at work.

Tom turned on the TV and stood there while the tubes warmed up. His adoptive father was born in Poughkeepsie and had been a Giants' fan even after his family moved to Johnstown on his dad's tenth birthday. Tom adopted his dad's team and stayed true to them even though he felt cheated when they moved to San Francisco when Tom was about that same age. It annoyed him when the Pittsburgh Pirates beat his Giants for the National League Pennant, so he switched his loyalties to the defending World Series champs from Baltimore. He made it clear to the guys at work that it was for the championship games only.

The Series had started out looking pretty good when the Orioles won the first two games at home, but yesterday the Bucs took the first of three at Three Rivers Stadium.

As the screen lit up, he tuned in the game and then settled into his recliner with a beer and pretzels. Tom's confidence came back when Baltimore went up by three runs in a first-inning eruption that saw the Pirates replace their starting pitcher only two outs into the game. A commercial came on, so Tom jumped up and ran to the kitchen to get another beer. Yep, tonight the O-birds were going to go up three games to one!

By the seventh inning, Tom was losing his confidence and his temper. The Pirates had scored four unanswered runs to take the lead. He sat in his chair and yelled at the TV as if to convince his temporary team to inflict the damage on his foes that his beloved Giants had not been able to do. As he sat during a commercial break, a promotion came on for the late local news program promising, among other things, a story about some war protestors in nearby Compton. The announcer said the protesters had called the soldiers "criminals" and were going to gather in the park at 10 o'clock that night to demonstrate their antiwar sentiments by burning their draft cards.

If the truck door aggravated Tom and the game had made him angry, the news blurb took him to the boiling point. He shouted at the moving images on the screen and then threw his bottle at the TV. It hit the edge of the wooden cabinet and shattered into pieces, spilling a mixture of beer and glass shards all over the floor.

Tom was incensed. "Maybe it's time they find out what it feels like to have a 'criminal' beat 'em to a pulp!" he hollered as he stormed out of the house. The truck door squawked as he yanked it open and got in.

He was shaking with rage. It took him three tries to get the key into the ignition switch. He revved the engine, pulled the transmission into gear, and popped the clutch throwing a dust cloud off the dirt driveway. The spinning tires tore up what little grass they had as he pulled through the yard and bounced out over the curb and onto the street.

Once on the road, he replayed the events of the evening over and over in his mind. His truck door, the game, the protesters—the only things he could think of were things that stirred his anger. He got out on the main road and opened it up. At times, the speeds scared even him, causing him to back down a little.

As Tom sped toward Compton, he approached Pete's Place on the left. That was his favorite bar. He decided to see if any of his buddies wanted to join in the fun of breaking some jaws. As he pulled in, he recognized Jerry's car and thought he spotted Drake's panel truck in the back of the lot.

Once inside, Tom found his buddies at their usual table in the back. He slung a chair around from another table and almost hit the wall with it.

"Whoa Tom, who burned your bacon?" Wally asked.

Tom let loose with a string of profanity loud enough to embarrass the others.

"Easy, buddy," Drake said in a low tone as if talking softly would somehow mitigate Tom's outburst.

"What are you talking about?" Jerry asked.

"They're on the TV calling me a criminal. *And I'm not!*" he said emphatically, still speaking too loudly for everyone's comfort.

Jerry waved a waitress to the table. "Ginger, get a beer for Tommy here." Then turning back to his friends, he said, "Let's talk this thing over and see what we can work out."

"We can work it out by busting some heads," Tom responded. "We need to go over to Compton tonight and teach a lesson to a bunch of wimps."

"Right," Jerry responded still trying to distract Tom enough so that he could reduce the rage. "But if we are going to bust some heads, we have to have a plan. Let's figure how we are going to pull this thing off."

Tom started in on his beer as soon as it hit the table, and Jerry gave a look to the other two that made it clear they needed to play along with him. Otherwise, this thing was going to get *way* out of control. He had seen Tom's hot temper before, but never had he seen his friend this upset.

Jerry liked sports but mostly bowling and football. He was not a big baseball fan, so he had not been watching the game. He didn't have any idea about the truck door, the game, or the news clip. Nor did he know the depth of the internal acids that were etching into Tom's very being. All he knew was that Tom was normally an okay guy for a hothead, but when he got out on the edge like this he turned into a fighting machine with an attitude. The best way to defuse this thing was to get Tom drunk and hope they could change the subject enough that he would forget what was gnawing at him.

Nine beers and two bathroom trips later, Tom was finally to the point where he was laughing and joking—way beyond wanting to hurt anybody. He was really tanked, and not only didn't remember *why* he had been angry, he didn't even remember that he *had* been angry. They sat with him awhile; then when they were sure he was too drunk to act on his emotions, they left one by one, hoping Tom wouldn't notice.

As the last to leave, Jerry stopped at the bar on his way out. "Ginger, could you get some coffee down Tommy before he tries to leave?"

"We close in forty minutes," she said. "I can't perform miracles."

"I know. I just think it would be best if we weren't here when he sobers up. So he doesn't remember what he was so mad about, ya know?"

"I'll do my best." She had witnessed Tom's initial outburst and had read between the lines. She appreciated what Jerry had done for Tom, but sobering him up would take enough coffee that another trip or two to the bathroom would be the result. She reached for the pot of coffee they brewed every night an hour or so before closing time.

~~~

At twenty minutes after closing time, Ginger finally convinced Tom it was time to leave. The sudden chill of the October air startled Tom as he stepped outside. Somehow he did not remember anything else after that until he pulled into his driveway. The next thing he knew was waking up in the truck with the engine still running. He had no idea how long he had slept there.

He got out and stumbled toward the house. When he finally reached the door, he could not find his key. Where was the key? Then he noticed that his headlights were still on. As he went back to turn them off, he noticed that the truck was still running. He opened the door, reached in to switch off the ignition, and pulled out the keys. He closed the door and went back to the house, this time with keys in hand. Somehow, he managed to stagger to his room and collapse into bed.

~~~

Tom opened one eye. It sounded like a freight train was running through his bedroom, but if anyone else had been there they would not have heard it—the train was operating on a track that ran between Tom's ears.

He squinted at the alarm clock on the nightstand and could not understand why it was so light in the room if it was almost midnight. He must have forgotten to turn the light off. Yeah, that was it.

He pulled the covers over his head for a few moments, but then it began to dawn on him that the time was almost noon, not midnight. He recalled being at Pete's Place and probably had not even left there until after midnight.

Then it hit him: he was late for work! Again!

He thought about jumping out of bed but realized that jumping, or any other sudden movement, was something his pounding head would consider a bad idea.

He pulled the blanket back gently so as to not disturb the train too much. Slowly, he slid his legs over the side of the bed and sat up. The train began to accelerate. He pushed himself up off the bed and took slow, deliberate steps.

Once in the bathroom, he splashed some cold water onto his face trying to promote his return to reality. As he gained some stability in his legs, he got undressed and stepped into the shower.

What was he going to say to his boss? Gary Morgan was a fair man, but he insisted on a good day's work from his employees, and that included starting on time. Punctuality was not one of Tom's strengths. He had done well in the military when he was surrounded by other guys on the same schedule; when the motion started around him he could get into gear. However, once he was back at home Marsha had to nag and yell at him to get up. Even then, he had been late a number of times, particularly in the last several weeks. Now with her gone, he had been thirty minutes late on Monday, several minutes late on Tuesday and Wednesday, and would now be half of a day late!

Tom knew he was in for a lecture. "Well, let's get this over with," he muttered as he walked out of the house. He opened the truck door; the scraping reminded him of the accident down at the river. He got in and slammed the door angrily. He put the key in the ignition, but when he turned it, there was nothing. He had been distracted by the keys and had not turned out the lights when he went back to the truck last night—or this morning, whenever it was.

Tom's frustration was building again, so he sat there for a few minutes, trying to calm down. He finally got out of the truck, slammed the door again, and started the three-mile trek to the shop.

~~~

"You can't do that Mr. Morgan. I really need this job."

"I know, Tom, but I need someone I can count on." Gary was a wiz at business planning. He was also good with people, so when he had to take some kind of action, he was careful not to embarrass or belittle anyone. He just stuck with the facts. "Look, Tom, you need a job, and I need work done. Keeping you on gives you what you need but doesn't help me. I sell the services and products from my employees to my customers. That's how I get money to pay you and the others. But, if someone is not pulling his own weight, then it puts everything out of whack."

There was a pause. Tom knew that he had promised many times over that he would not to be late again, so he didn't know what to say. Finally Gary said, "I'll tell you what. I'll pay you for an extra week to help while you look for something else. I'll have Connie put your pay together. You can stop by tomorrow and pick it up."

After another long pause, Gary said, "I'm sorry, Tom. I really am. You're a nice guy, but this just isn't working out." He walked over and opened his office door. The shop noise which had been in the background suddenly flooded into the small room. After a moment, Tom slowly turned and walked toward the door. He didn't look up at Gary. He knew his boss—well, former boss—was doing what any manager would do and had probably given Tom more breaks than most others would have. He still didn't like it.

"Don't forget to stop by tomorrow," Gary reminded him.

"All right."

~~~

As Tom walked home, he wondered what he was going to do. Money was tight already; this was just going to make matters worse. Marsha was coming home from the tour tomorrow night, and she was going to explode.

When he got home, he ran an extension cord to the truck for the battery charger. The little metal box emitted a hum when he plugged it in; small sparks jumped off the second clamp when he connected it to the battery terminal. As it was charging, he walked out to the curb and pulled several letters from the mailbox.

All the way home he had pondered the events of the past several hours; now he continued to go through the what-if and the what-now scenarios. Once inside the house, he went into the kitchen and tossed the mail onto the table spilling an envelope onto the floor. He pulled a beer out of the refrigerator and opened it, then stooped to pick up the letter that had fallen. As he prepared to flip it back onto the table, he noticed that it had a handwritten Army P.O. box as the return address. Tom looked more closely. It was from his friend Larry Pullman who had been with Tom in the village ambush.

Tom set his beer down on the table and tore the envelope open.

"Hey, Tom," Larry began. "I'll be getting short before too long. Another month and a half and I will kiss this place goodbye FOREVER!" Tom grinned. He knew the feeling. "I'm looking forward to getting back to the good old US of A. I don't think I will ever be so glad to leave any place as much as I will be to leave here. Johnstown is a long way from Schenectady, but I'll look you up if I ever get over that way. By the way, they approved my R&R the week after you shipped out. I found that bar you told me about and stopped in to see how Trung Linh was doing like you asked me to. The guy at the bar said she was hit by a car and was killed several weeks ago. I even showed him the picture you left me to make sure. He said it was her. Sorry to have bad news; I could tell by the way you talked about her that you liked her and that she wasn't just someone you spent time with. Also, sorry I didn't get back to you before, but we've been out on patrols. Well, they're calling for chow. Got to go. Larry."

Tom didn't get through it all; his mind shut down just after "killed several weeks ago". He had spent a lot of time thinking of Linh since his return, especially after his arguments with Marsha. Why had he not asked her to go to Ceylon with him? His thoughts went back to Hong Kong and the time they spent together. His mind became a flood of memories, regrets, and guilt—the alley restaurant, the times at the park, at the museum, on the ferry, in the shops, the camera .... The camera!

Thoughts of the camera brought Tom back from the tumultuous sea of memories. He went down into the basement where he moved two small suitcases to the floor and slid a stack of old magazines out of the way. Reaching to the back of the shelf, he pulled out a shoebox. He looked at it for a moment then took the box up to the living room where he put it on the coffee table.

For almost an hour, he sat on the couch surrounded by small paper memories. Most of his Vietnam pictures, including some of his time in Hong Kong, were on a shelf there in the living room, but he did not dare leave this box of memories out where Marsha might see them. It was partially from shame and guilt and partially from not wanting to increase the volatility of the war zone that his home had become. Many of the pictures were innocent enough; the only thing that would have raised suspicion was that Linh was in every one of them. But there were others with the two of them holding hands or with his arm around her. And then there were other photos of her— less innocent ones.

One by one, he looked at the pictures; each triggered its own memory of the oasis those few days had been. She had been a friend to him. After he left Hong Kong, and particularly after his homecoming, her memories provided a fantasy that he liked to visit to escape his troubles. Now the young friend who he had remembered in his darkest moments was *only* that ... a memory. He would never see her again. She was gone. He felt like someone had pulled the plug on the only bright light that he had left in his life.

Eventually, his rememberer had remembered more than he wanted to remember. He went to the kitchen to get another beer. He only had three bottles left, but somehow, this just didn't feel like a three-bottle night.

He picked up his keys from the table and slowly walked out into the yard, leaves rustling underneath his feet. The events of the day were more than he could stand. He hung his head and wept. Warm tears quickly cooled in the October chill as they traced his cheeks and then fell to the ground.

Tom walked over to the truck, more on autopilot than deliberately. He got in, put the key in the ignition, and turned it. Unlike at noon, the engine turned over and fired up. He disconnected the charger, set it on the porch, got back into the truck, and sat there thinking for a few minutes. He did not want to go to Pete's Place where his friends hung out; he wanted to be alone. He put the truck in gear and headed out, not sure where he would end up.

Tom drove around with no destination in mind. He reviewed the memories that had permeated his thoughts as he sat with the pictures of a past that now had no future. Occasionally, he was reminded by horn blasts from several passing cars that his mind was not on his driving. He finally remembered a place over in Carson's Mill and decided to go there. In a few minutes, he was on the main highway headed for a tall mug and thinking that tomorrow had hangover written all over it.

~~~

"Anyone ready for another one?" the waitress called to each table as she walked around the room. Tom raised his hand to signal for another beer and took the last gulp of the one he was just finishing. He was right that he would drink more than three beers. But he had been there a little over six hours, and as best as he could recall, this new one would only be his fifth.

He was shaken and deeply saddened to learn of Linh's death. Reminiscing about their time together somehow took some of the edge off the tragic news. As the hours passed, his memories banked a warm fire in his heart, a luxury that his anger had not afforded him for a long time. However, he also began to realize that the fantasy-escape he took with Linh's memories anytime reality was not what he wanted allowed him to drift even further from the only life he actually had.

But more than that, Linh's death had also raised an increasing awareness of his own mortality. Only months ago, he was halfway around the world being shot at; here at home he drove recklessly and operated, or used to operate, dangerous machines. "I was lucky to get out of The Nightmare alive," he thought. A list of names rotated through his mind of buddies whose luck had run out on foreign soil.

The warm thoughts of the past mingled with the more sobering aspects of the present caused Tom to reflect on his life and whatever future it might still hold. The result was that he spent more time thinking than drinking.

"I can do better than this," he said quietly to himself. "I need to start putting my life back together. Maybe I better get home and straighten up the place. She's gonna be back tomorrow, and I haven't cleaned all week." He thought for another minute, finished his beer, and made a trip to the men's room before leaving.

~~~

It was dark, almost ten o'clock. Tom could not remember the last time he had left a bar that early or that sober. He had contemplated what he was going to do and made a decision based on the way things really were. Now he was driving home to start a completely new life.

On the way home, he stopped at a carryout to pick up a couple cartons of beer. He reasoned with himself that he needed to drink less, but it wouldn't hurt to have some around the house. He also realized that he had missed today's game, but game six was on Saturday and he needed to make sure he had some beer on hand.

It was only four miles from the carryout to the house. All the way home he thought of the changes he was going to make; it felt good to start taking charge of his life.

He slowed quickly as he approached the driveway. There was Marsha's car. His headlights swung around as he turned in, and he saw her behind the wheel. Just then she turned on her lights and pulled the gearshift down. He was not sure what to do, nor did he have any idea why she was home. The next moment, she swung out to the side lurching around him and out onto the street almost hitting his truck.

Tom sat there for a moment waiting for his heart to go back down into his chest. What in the world was that all about? Then his heart almost stopped when he suddenly realized that he had not put away those pictures.

"What is she doing home today? I thought this was Thursday. Or is it Friday? No, it's Thursday. If I had just not gone to the bar! If I had just come home earlier..."

Questions and alternatives flowed into his mind like water into the Niagara Falls basin. He sat in the truck, stunned and motionless, wishing he could take back the last six hours. Finally, he came to his senses. The door creaked as he got out of the truck; he was so shaken he didn't even notice. As he walked toward the house, he noticed the light from the open doorway illuminated something yellow in the front yard. He picked it up. It was one of Marsha's favorite dresses.

He looked up at the house. He could see through the open door, through the living room and into the kitchen. One of the dinette chairs had been tipped over, and the mail was on the floor. As he entered the house, he looked to the side; his photographs were scattered all over the living room. Some were crumpled while others' were torn into pieces. The pictures looked like they had been shot out of a cannon. They were on the floor, on the mantle, on the recliner, on the couch, up on the back of the couch—everywhere. The box he had kept them in sat in a corner with the side crushed in.

He was sick to his stomach. He had feared that this day might come, and it had. With a vengeance! He gathered the pictures and pieces together and put them back into the box, straightening out the caved-in side. As best as he could, he smoothed out the pictures Marsha had crumpled.

By this time, Tom was on slow-motion autopilot. He noticed a chill and closed the front door. Then he went into the kitchen where he found Larry's letter in tatters. He gathered up the pieces and placed them and the envelope in the box.

He went into the bedroom. The closet door was open, most of her clothes were gone, and all of his were on the floor. He stood there motionless for a moment, then walked to the bed, pulled back the covers and lay down, fully dressed, shoes and all. He pulled the covers over himself as warm moisture filled his eyes.

He turned onto his side and clutched the box to his chest. All of his thoughts of a better life had evaporated now; despair would be his only companion tonight.

~~~

"Hi, Marsha. Come in." Violet could hear the strain in her voice when Marsha called earlier. "It didn't take you long to get here."

"Thanks, Vi. I was packed before I called," Marsha replied with the same strain in her voice. Now that she was here, Violet could see the tension on her face too.

"The guest room is ready; it's right up the hall." She took the suitcase from Marsha and led the way. "The bathroom is right here across from your room," she said as she turned into the bedroom. Violet turned on the light and opened the closet door. In several moves, they had hung up the armful of clothes Marsha brought from home.

"You didn't have any trouble finding the house?"

"No, your directions were good."

The sentences were short, and the hour was late. "I guess we both better get some sleep," Vi said.

"Yeah," Marsha replied. "That would be good."

"Not to pry, but you were supposed to be gone all week. Has that changed? I mean, are you going in to work tomorrow?"

"No, Aunt Renee didn't feel well, so she and I skipped the last concert and came home early, but I have some things that I need to do tomorrow."

"Okay. There is an alarm clock on the stand next to the bed if you want it. I have some tests at the hospital tomorrow, so I took the day off. I'll be getting up around seven. I can wake you up when the coffee is ready if you want."

"That would be good. Thanks."

"Okay. Good night."

"Good night."

~~~

As desperately as he wished, sleep would not come to Tom this night. He lay there for a half hour then finally decided to get up. He slowly walked out into the living room and over to the recliner. As he sat there, the list of messes in his life played through his mind like a jukebox: the job loss, Marsha moving out, Linh's death ....

Amidst all his thoughts—and without warning—all of the sights and all of the sounds of The Nightmare came rushing to the surface as if his mind were a boiling cauldron churning up the memories of everything that had happened to him. Shooting and explosions and noises and flashes and yelling and screaming and hurt and death—it was all a huge mixture from which it was impossible to separate one repugnant detail from another.

There was that time when he was playing cards with Mike Gentry and they came to tell Mike that his brother had died in a skirmish just a dozen kilometers away. Then there was the time when that goat wandered into their camp and distracted them, so the two VCs almost surprised them. And then there was the ambush just outside the village.

Even the memory of smells was vivid: the jungle, the gunpowder, the sweat, the stench of death. Everything that he had struggled to forget these last few months was now rushing through his mind like a torrent. It was as if a dam had broken and the floodwaters were careening downhill carrying his wounds through his mind, carving out new gashes as they went—painful gashes.

Then there was his time with Linh. "I can't believe she's dead," he thought as he shook his head slightly. Slowly the words escaped his lips. Not deliberately, they just came out. "I wish I had asked her to go away with me."

Slowly, he lay back in the recliner and closed his eyes as if to block out the upheaval. Eyelids are good shutters to prevent new things from entering the mind, but Tom found them totally useless against the onslaught of the memories which his mind already contained.

"Isn't once enough for a nightmare?" he whispered through clenched teeth. "Do I have to keep living it over and over?"

A deep despair began to press down as if someone was sitting on his chest. It was a feeling that he had not known for a while. He had struggled with this foe occasionally during The Nightmare and several times since he returned. He was in for another round; he would be the loser again.

Bit by bit, almost as if rising from a jungle mist, the word alone materialized in his mind. Not just lonely—*alone*. ALL alone. It was all gone —his parents, his wife, his job, Linh—all gone. With Marsha gone and no job, he would soon have no home; he would have to move out of the house.

For the first time in his life, there was little that he could think of as his own and even less to live for. "Why?" he asked. "Why did it happen like this? Why was I even born? I was just an unwanted baby. I finally had parents who loved me, and then they died. I found somebody to marry, then The Nightmare wrecked my life and I wrecked my marriage. Why?" Then with more anger and through clenched teeth, he yelled, "*WHY*?!"

The more he thought, the more he wanted not to think. The more he wanted not to think, the more he thought. "Funny how that works," he reflected.

Suddenly he remembered his gun.

~~~

Slowly, Violet Thompson woke up. Sunlight was starting to poke its fingers through the edge of the curtains, so she knew she had slept a lot later than she usually did even for a day off.

She put on her bathrobe and slippers. As steadily as she could, Vi stumbled down the hall to the kitchen. She was a slave to that little South American coffee bean, and she needed a 'fix'. Her husband Victor teased her about her habit, even 'lamenting' his role in being her 'pusher' anytime she asked him to pick up some of her auburn dust at the store. He asked her if she had ever considered just setting up an IV drip in the morning, but the only reward he got for his suggestion was *the look* so he didn't mention it again. At least not too often.

Soon the aroma of the South American bean juice filled the kitchen and began wafting into the living room where Violet had laid down on the couch waiting for the magic potion to brew. She slowly got up and moved into the kitchen where she poured a tall cup of the dark fluid that would soon restore her to normalcy.

Victor had been out on the West Coast for three months supervising an installation. He only came back every third weekend. Marsha worked with Violet and had mentioned the trouble she and Tom were having. Victor and Violet had talked about Marsha staying in the guest bedroom while she tried to sort things out. Their daughter and her husband came for a visit every several months and had been there last weekend while Victor was home. The young couple would not likely be back for a while, so they had agreed that Marsha could use the guestroom if it came to that. Last night it came to that; just before bedtime, Marsha had called asking if she could take advantage of Violet's offer.

After she drank half a cup, Violet poured it full again and then filled a second cup and headed back up the hall, both cups in tow. As she came to the guest bedroom, she reached out one of the cups to tap gently on the door but drew it back when she heard muffled crying. Amidst the sobs were words, but Violet could not make them out.

After a few moments, it occurred to her she was invading private space; she quietly backed away and returned to the kitchen.

Violet poured the second cup back into the coffee pot and took her cup to the couch to sip her delightful medicine and await her guest's appearance.

After a time, Violet heard stirring. Eventually, the guestroom door opened, and Marsha came down the hall.

"Coffee is on the stove," Violet volunteered.

"Thanks," Marsha responded turning into the kitchen. She re-emerged with a steaming cup and sat down in the easy chair.

"I'm going out looking for apartments today," Marsha said.

"So soon?" Violet asked. "I thought you were just *thinking* about leaving Tom." She took another sip.

Marsha was hurt and angry, but deep down she was still not sure she would actually go through with a divorce. However, without mentioning the specific events of last night, she responded, "I know, but I am tired of him, and I'm tired of all that he is putting me through. I am *waaay* too tired to keep this up any longer. I need to know what apartments are out there; I guess I am not going to find out until I look."

It got quiet. Marsha thought about what she had said. Her "waaay too tired" speech was exactly how she felt, but the way she had said it was terse. Her hostess did not deserve that. She apologized, and Violet accepted graciously.

After she finished her cup of coffee, Marsha walked back to the kitchen and poured some more. Returning to the doorway, she asked if Violet subscribed to the newspaper.

"Yes, it should be on the front porch. You can have it."

"Thank you," Marsha said politely.

After retrieving the paper, she spread it out on the kitchen table and began looking through the apartment ads.

~~~

Tom had gotten his gun last night and loaded it. Then he had laid back in the recliner to contemplate his last moments on earth. He was tired of his life, tired of the wreck that he had made of it, and just plain tired.

He awoke with the gun on his chest where he had left it; he had not stirred all night.

He remembered the despair of the night before. He was still upset but did not feel as helpless as he had just hours before. He certainly did not feel bad enough to end his life just yet. He always had that option, but for now, he needed a beer.

Tom unloaded the revolver, put the shells back in the box, and placed the box and the pistol on the top shelf in the hall closet. Then he went to the refrigerator and wrapped his hand around the neck of a tall, cold bottle. He popped the top off in a motion that spilled a little of the golden sauce. "Life is never so complicated that a beer won't help," he said with a chuckle. Later, he might just go fishing. "Yeah, that would be good—fishing and some cold beer."

~~~

Marsha circled five apartment possibilities. She knew where three of them were, and Violet knew about one of the others. Marsha put her cup in the sink, gathered up the newspaper, and went down the hall to get ready. In another thirty minutes, she was walking out the door. She wanted to take a driving tour so that she would know something about the neighborhoods before she actually contacted an agent.

~~~

Within an hour, Tom was sitting on the bank at his favorite fishing spot. The temperature was unseasonably warm for an autumn day. He could imagine the fish keeping him busy all day.

The fish started hitting quickly. Soon Tom had a catfish on his stringer. Within five minutes, he had another. Then the activity slowed down. He relaxed, awaiting the next catch.

While he waited, Tom began to think of the events of the last couple of days. He wondered where Marsha had gone. Since she had taken almost all her clothes, he suspected that she didn't have plans to come back anytime soon. How he had gotten to where he was and how the future was likely to unfold were thoughts that would increasingly occupy his mind in the days that lay before him.

After another hour with no more activity, Tom packed up his gear and headed back home. He put the fish away and then cleaned up to go looking for a job. None of the places were hiring. A nearby car dealership needed a salesman, but he had no experience in sales and didn't want that kind of work anyway. He said he did mechanical work, and they took his information just in case something opened up in the service department.

Back home, he cooked one of the fish and sat down to watch some TV.

~~~

Marsha's weekend consisted of driving from place to place looking at apartments and neighborhoods. None interested her from the outside. Either the areas were not what she had in mind, or they were just too far from work. When Monday rolled around, she dragged herself out of bed. Violet had the coffee ready again. Since they worked together, they decided to take just one car.

Once at her desk, the emotion of the past several days started to surface. She was able to do her work, but several times, tears filled her eyes and spilled out onto her face.

During the past few weeks, her girl-talk had not been confined to Violet, so Sandra put the pieces together when she saw the moist eyes. "Men are such jerks," she blurted out. "You'll be better off without him. That's why I dumped Carter."

Embarrassed, Marsha got up from her desk and excused herself to the bathroom. Closing the door to the stall, she pulled off a length of tissue and sat down for a long cry. "What happened to Tom?" she thought. "What happened to us? What happened to *me*?"

She sat with her head in her hands, flipping questions through her mind as if they were on a key ring ... one, then another, followed by another. As she grew increasingly tired of the unanswered rotation, she heard the roll of approaching thunder. The mood for the day was set.

~~~

After being discharged from the service, Glenn Abney stopped by his sister's place in Oregon for a couple of weeks. Before leaving, he decided he would visit the Grand Canyon on his way back to Johnstown. From everything he read, he thought the south rim would give him the best views, and fantastic views they were too! He had heard about the canyon all his life and had viewed many pictures, but looking at something so vast in magazines and books is like envisioning a skyscraper by looking at blueprints for a birdhouse. He was awed with the magnitude of the site and glad he went out of his way to see it.

A smile crossed his face when he recalled the story he heard as a child about Paul Bunyan creating the canyon by dragging his ax. "You sure was usin' some big ol' ax there, Mr. Bunyan," he said in his Texas drawl as he inspected the huge cavity in the earth's crust.

Glenn stopped at several places and surveyed the vast domain from a number of vantage points. He slept out under the stars several nights. The clear skies drew his mind back to what his sister had said. She hadn't been mean about it. On the contrary, she seemed genuinely concerned. Glenn could not get it out of his mind, but he couldn't quite get his mind around it either.

~~~

Marsha couldn't sleep. She looked at the clock on the nightstand and remembered a coworker once wisecracking, "I never knew there were two five o'clocks in the same day!"

"Yeah, me too," she quipped as she snapped the covers back and got out of bed.

She moved about quietly not wanting to awaken Violet. After getting ready, she left a note for her friend. Five minutes later, she was on the way to work. She was not usually this early, but she hadn't gotten much done the last several days and had some catching up to do.

~~~

Several weeks went by. Tom continued to look for work, but there wasn't much available. Or maybe it was just that his reputation as a lackadaisical hothead was getting out there ahead of him. Either way, his time was shared between unsuccessful job searches, mostly-successful fishing expeditions, and always-successful attempts to fall asleep watching television with a beer nearby.

~~~

Marsha pulled into the parking lot. She had finally found an apartment listing that interested her and had driven by it the night before on her way to meet the girls for their Friday night outing.

Standing on the sidewalk was a handsome, middle-aged man in a suit and tie. As she pulled up to the curb, he stepped over to her car.

"Marsha?" he asked.

"Yes."

"Hi, I'm Lamont Jackson," he said stretching out his hand. "We spoke on the phone this morning."

"Hi. Marsha Jenkins." They shook hands through the open window.

"So, this is it, huh?" she said getting out of the car.

"Yes. Apartment Four is on the end of this building here," he said, motioning to the structure behind him. "As I mentioned on the phone, this is one of the nicer areas on this side of town. It has good schools; it's close to shopping and only a fifteen-minute drive to town. Didn't you say you work in the Wallstone Building?"

"Yes. This wouldn't be a bad drive."

"Great!" Lamont commented. "Let's take a look inside."

As they approached the door, she glanced over the area. The building and parking lot seemed to be in good shape. The lawn was manicured, and the hedges were well attended. Marsha's mother was a real estate agent and had taught Marsha how to identify a well-cared-for property.

The apartment was modest but homey. They had repainted it and installed new carpet after the previous tenants moved out.

Lamont began the tour. As Marsha walked around, she began to sense that this place could be her home for a time. There was an excitement in that realization, but it was a bittersweet, almost hollow excitement. Whether it was a sense of guilt or apprehension or something else, a whole jarful of butterflies had made their way into her stomach.

They finished the tour and headed out the front door. Lamont locked up and walked Marsha back to the parking lot where they talked for a few minutes. She told him that she liked the place but that she needed to check her budget; she would have to get back to him. After a few more words, they shook hands and each headed back to their cars.

Chapter 3 – Holidays Alone

The thought of spending Thanksgiving alone was depressing to Tom, but things were what they were. He stepped outside and found that it was warm enough that the fish might bite, so he decided to go down by the river and try his luck. He got dressed, grabbed his keys, and headed out the door. He always kept his fishing gear in the truck, just in case.

After his fishing venture yielded two medium-sized catfish, "a profitable endeavor," he thought to himself, Tom headed back home to clean the fish and throw one in the freezer. He would cook the other one for supper.

As he showered, he remembered that the big Nebraska game was today. Everybody had been talking about it all week, and it promised to be a good contest. He dressed and then stopped in the kitchen for another beer and some pretzels. This was going to be a good day after all.

Tom walked into the living room where he turned on the TV, tuned in the game, and then settled back in the recliner to get ready for the action. Halfway through the first quarter, he was sound asleep, pretzels in his lap and a beer on the end table beside him. The stress of his fears and anxieties had taken their toll, even while he relaxed on the riverbank. The beer had not helped him stay awake either.

Fifteen minutes later, a car drove into the driveway. Marsha had decided to stop by and pick up the rest of her things. She really didn't want to have to face Tom and hoped that someone had invited him for Thanksgiving dinner. But there was that old truck. She could see damage to the driver's side door that she hadn't seen before. "I'm sure I didn't hit it when I drove around him that night," she tried to assure herself.

After a delay she mumbled, "This isn't going to get done by itself." Marsha opened the car door and got out. As she reached the house, she almost rang the bell, but then she stopped short remembering that this was her house too. At least some of her things were still here. She drew in a breath of bravery and opened the door.

The TV was on as she walked in and glanced over at the recliner.

"Drunk as usual," she muttered under her breath. Half of her was angry. The other half was relieved that she might be able to get in and out of the house without a confrontation.

Marsha moved quickly but quietly. Soon she was back on the road with the rest of her clothes and the photo album she forgot to take when she moved to the Thompson's.

~~~

There was a noise—a ringing. It was the phone. Tom got up and almost tripped on the way to the kitchen.

"Hello," he managed to get out.

"Tommy! Did you see the game?" It was Wally, one of his drinking buddies.

"Uh … well … actually I fell asleep. What happened?"

"Aw you missed it, Tommy. It was Kinney. A hundred and seventy one yards for four TDs. It was awesome, man! What a game! You just know he's gonna get picked in the first round next year. Probably Tagge too," he added, referring to the Nebraska quarterback.

Tom's head was starting to clear. "Wow. What a game. I wished I had stayed awake."

"We're going over to Pete's Place to celebrate. Are you comin'?"

"Yeah," Tommy said. "Yeah. I'll meet you there in a little bit."

Tom hung up the phone and put the pretzels on the counter. He chugged another swallow of his opened beer and then decided he had better visit the bathroom before he took off. He really had drunk a lot of beer since breakfast.

~~~

Tom looked around and saw Jerry, Wally, and Drake sitting at their favorite table back in the corner. He walked over and greeted them.

"Hey, Tommy, how's it going, buddy?" Jerry asked. Tom pulled out a chair next to Wally who reached over and gave him a guy-punch as he sat down.

"It's okay, I guess," he replied to Jerry's question. To Jerry, it was a general greeting; however, in his frame of mind, Tom thought of it as a personal inquiry. "Marsha still hasn't come back," he lamented. "I haven't seen her since she left, and I don't even know where she is. I try to call her at work, but I always get cut off. I just …"

While he struggled for the words to finish the sentence, Drake choked down a swallow of beer and blurted out, "Yeah, my ol' lady is

50

always mad at me too. That's why I come here to get away from her nagging all the time."

The waitress stopped by the table and asked Tom if he wanted a beer. "Yeah. Thanks, Ginger." She returned with a mug of brew.

Tom sat there sipping his beer. The guys were talking, but Tom's mind was somewhere else. He was still wondering how he had gotten so far off track and what he could do to get things straightened out. "So far off track," he thought.

Someone called his name, but the voice just mixed in with everything else in his mind. "TOM!" Ginger called out again. This time, Tom looked up. "You have a phone call." Then, just moving her mouth, "It's your wife."

"Ooooh" came from all three friends at the same time. "She found ya, Tommy."

"Yeah, there just ain't no place to hide as long as there's a telephone around."

As he walked to the bar, he was not sure what he was going to say. She was going to be angry that he was drinking again. Then he had a thought ... he would just say he wasn't drinking, that he was just talking with his friends. Yeah, that was it: they were drinking, but he wasn't.

After a couple minutes, he returned to the table. "I gotta go," he announced. "We're meeting at The Ranch."

The oooooohs started again, but Tom just headed for the door. "She's gotcha, Tommy. She found ya, and she gotcha," he heard them call. He just kept walking. At least there was hope or she wouldn't have called.

~~~

The Ranch was a locally owned family steak house. It was a new place when Tom and Marsha started going together, so they went there on their first date. It quickly became one of their favorite places for a casual dinner.

The Ranch had not been open on Thanksgiving before today. The manager decided to try it this year and advertised the fact on the radio. The experiment had been a reasonable success with a good flow of traffic earlier, but now the restaurant was not even as full as on a regular night.

Tom pulled into the parking lot and drove to the back. He didn't see Marsha's car and figured it might be smart to size up the situation first. He was not sure why he thought that; he just did.

A few minutes later, Marsha drove up. A car up front had just left, and she pulled into the space. Tom watched as she got out and walked toward the door. She was a good distance away, and he could not see her well; however, for some reason, he got the impression that she was not in a particularly good frame of mind.

He began to reason that he was just not in the mood for another lecture. "I've had all of that I can stand," he said quietly as he turned the key and started the engine. He sat there briefly, but after a few moments, his craving to have her back overcame his pride and fears. He turned the engine off and got out of the truck.

Marsha was in the corner to the far left facing the door. Tom walked back and sat down across the table from her. They each said, "Hi." Marsha set the menu down as the waiter walked up with her tea.

"What can I get you to drink, sir?" he asked.

"I'll have an RC Cola," Tom replied. "And I'll have a Porterhouse, medium rare, and a baked potato with butter."

"Yes, sir. And for the lady?"

"I would like the turkey dinner," she said, "and a salad with Italian dressing please."

"Very good," the waiter said as he picked up the menus. "I'll put that order right in."

Their conversation was stilted small-talk. Soon Marsha started to smell beer. She questioned him, and he said, "It's like I told you. They were drinking, but I wasn't. I just got there a minute before you called." He had gotten good at making things up as he went along. Besides, it was true that he hadn't been there long.

She leaned forward and angrily whispered, "Well, they weren't drinking that beer you had while you were watching the game this afternoon."

He sat there looking down at the table. How did she know about that?

The waiter brought her salad.

"Look," Marsha finally said. "I think we need to be separated for a while."

"That's what we have now," he shot back, still annoyed at her accusations.

Things suddenly got cold—colder, actually—and the conversation stopped. The food came, and they ate in silence. She had only eaten a little of the salad and a bite or two of the turkey when she reached for her purse and put some money on the table.

"This was a bad idea," she said. She got up and headed for the door.

Tom was embarrassed. She had never walked out on him in public before. As she walked past him, his eyes followed her reflection in the window that had been behind her. She walked out the door and with her, all his thoughts that maybe there was hope.

He sat there motionless for a few minutes thinking about the past and the present. He had come to grips with the reality that there was no future with Linh and that there probably never had been. Now he was starting to realize that there was likely no future with Marsha either.

When enough time had passed that he was sure she was out of the parking lot, he picked up the check and her money. Laying down a tip, he headed toward the counter where he paid the bill and started to leave.

"Hi, Tom," he heard from behind. He turned to see Frank Richards, a high school buddy whom he had not seen since his homecoming. He was a year ahead of Tom in school, but they had been friends. During his senior year, Frank started working at Lansing's Gas and Service. When Mr. Lansing retired early last year, Frank bought the station and renamed it FRANK'S GARAGE.

"You remember my wife Debbie," Frank said putting his arm around behind her.

Debbie smiled and reached out. "Sure," Tom said, shaking her hand. "You always were the lucky one, Frank."

Debbie got a shy grin on her face and said, "Thank you, Tom. That's sweet."

"You're right, Tom. Debbie is the perfect wife for me," Frank replied as he looked into her smiling face.

"Say, Tom, I hear you got laid off at Morgan's place." Before Tom could reply, Frank continued. "Robbie Thomas used to work for me, but his mom is having trouble with her hip. He moved back to Memphis last week to take care of her. I could sure use some help at the station."

At first, Tom was not sure he had heard correctly. His mind reeled at the thought of an unsolicited job offer. He had been looking for weeks with not so much as a spark of interest. A job dropping out of the sky caught him off guard. When he regained his thoughts, he said, "Hey, Frank … yeah, that would be great. What's the deal?"

"Well, come by tomorrow morning before eight, and we can talk."

"Sure!" Tom responded. "Thanks. Thanks a lot!"

Tom shook Frank's hand again, said his goodbyes, walked out the door, and started toward his truck. It did not seem like as long a walk as it had been just a half hour before.

~~~

Tom stopped by Pete's Place on the way home to see if the guys were still there. They were.

"Hey, Tommy," Jerry called out. "We're gonna go bowling. You still got your stuff in the truck?"

"I can't guys. I just saw Frank Richards, and I think he's gonna give me a job. I got to go over there early in the morning."

"Oh, Tommy, forget him. Let's go bowling."

"Come on, Tommy."

"Yeah, Frank is a loser just like Marsha."

Tom was still upset with Marsha. This wasn't helping, so he finally just turned around and walked out. The chatter and noise from his friends continued until he was out the door. After that, he didn't care what they said.

~~~

Victor had come home for Thanksgiving.

"Hi, Victor," Marsha said as she walked through the door. He returned the greeting and asked if she had a nice dinner.

"Well, not exactly. It was with Tom, so I should have known it wouldn't work out."

Victor did not respond; he didn't know what to say. He was a very personable man and quite wise for his forty-five years, but he simply had no point of reference for Marsha's plight. Violet and he had been sweethearts since their mid-teens; they married when they were both eighteen, and next month they would celebrate twenty-seven years of what he called "the perfect marriage to the perfect princess."

"I'm sorry if my remarks were rude," she said. Victor assured her that he was not offended. Marsha dismissed herself and headed to her room for the night.

Tom awoke with a gasp and began coughing on the droplets of moisture that his breath had drawn into his lungs. His first waking thoughts continued the panic from his dream—a dream that he was late. "Wha .... What time is it?" he thought, looking at the clock. This was the third time ... no, the fourth time he had awakened with the same dream.

His night had been one long dread that his alarm clock would not go off, or that he would not hear it, or that he would shut it off and go back to sleep. Now it was almost time to get up anyway.

As he sat on the edge of the bed trying to recover from the latest scare, the alarm *did* go off startling him with its loud clattering. Tom reached over to silence the alarm. "That's why I hate those things," Tom thought. "They scare you half to death, and when you lay down to recover from all of the racket, you just go back to sleep anyway."

The concern of not waking in time to meet with Frank had been part of his fear since he had been fired from his last job because of his tardiness. However, Tom's continuous anxiety had been building for years now, and it had more at its center than a fear of ignoring an alarm clock. His angst was the result of a life of following his own way—"doing your own thing" his generation called it. Tom had been doing his own thing for years and had the inner turmoil to prove it.

His childhood years were rough. He sometimes blamed his actions on his beginnings, but even he had to admit that after Marion and Lindsay Jenkins adopted him he had a reasonably good life. Still, there were things he knew should never have happened. He knew he did things that upset them and had done even more that they never knew about. At least, he *hoped* they never knew.

Then after his dad's boating accident, he *really* started making bad choices. Some of them were genuine mistakes, decisions he made without thinking things through. However, others were careless or foolish choices he had made against his own better judgment which alienated those around him. It was not just his choice with Linh. There were angry outbursts, abusive words, hostilities, bitterness, dishonesty ... the kinds of things that affect a person's life long after the act itself.

It often angered him that people had stopped forgiving him. What really troubled him was the slow realization that he had stopped forgiving himself. The human spirit can endure a lot. Someone else not forgiving you is hard to take, but you not forgiving yourself is almost impossible to bear.

~~~

Tom stood at the mirror lathering his face. He chuckled to himself that this was the first time he had shaved in three days. He didn't know why that struck him as funny, it just did; maybe because he was nervous. He never liked the idea of having a beard, so he was not trying to start one; he just had not taken the time to shave.

He finished his shaving ritual and hopped into the shower. In a few minutes, he was out and getting dressed.

One thought that crossed his mind was that the job was not a done deal; he was going for an interview. He realized he knew that all along, but it had not really occurred to him until now. "I sure hope Frank hires me," he thought as he finished buttoning his shirt, combed his hair, and headed out the door.

~~~

There was Frank's place up ahead on the right. He looked at his watch; it was 7:30. "Frank said before eight, and 7:30 is before eight," he thought to himself with another grin. That was the second time this morning that he had found humor in something which others would have found mundane. Everything seemed right. This was going to be a good day, and Tom had not had one of those in a really long time.

The bell rang as Tom drove his truck into the station. Frank walked out to greet him. They chatted for a few minutes, and then the conversation turned to work. "Well, I told you that Robbie moved to Memphis, so I really need a good mechanic, and I know that you used to work on cars. I really need someone who will be focused and dependable, someone who can help me serve our customers."

"I know," Tom said. "I'll try."

Frank paused. "I don't need you to try, Tom. I need someone who can do it." Frank's look was not unkind, but Tom could tell that dependability was important to Frank.

"Okay. I can do that."

"Good. Can you start today?"

"Sure," Tom said with a smile.

"All right," Frank said through a smile of his own. "Robbie was a little bigger than you are, but you can wear his shirts until I get you some."

Tom took off his shirt, put on Robbie's, and started buttoning it up.

"The Buick over in the far bay needs an oil change and a radiator flush. The work order is on the dashboard." Frank explained his practice of writing down the things he did on a filing card so he could keep a history of each car, a trick he had learned from Mr. Lansing when he first started there.

Tom felt like he was floating as he walked over to the car, set the hoist pads, and began to lift the car into the air.

~~~

Marsha sat nervously at the table. She was actually going through with it. "The Big Step," she thought to herself.

Lamont came back with the rental papers and sat on the other side of the table.

"Sorry I kept putting you off," she said. "I just had trouble making up my mind."

"That's all right," he replied. "I'm just glad that the apartment is still available. I thought for sure that place would be rented before now."

He explained all of the clauses, what was covered and what was not. The apartment owners had insurance on the building, but she should have insurance on the things that belonged to her ... she could put her garbage in the dumpster at the end of the parking lot ... pick up was on Wednesday afternoons ... And on it went...

Lamont prided himself on explaining things clearly, but like many young renters, Marsha only heard bits and pieces as her mind was on a number of other things. She had to leave soon to meet with the lawyer.

When the preliminaries were finished, it was time to sign the papers. Ten minutes later, Marsha was sitting in her car looking at a signed contract; her purse was two keys heavier.

~~~

Tom was surprised when Frank called out into the bays and told him it was six o'clock. "How was your first day?" he asked.

"I don't think I have ever had a day go by so fast."

"Yeah," Frank replied. "I find that a whole week can go by before I know it."

Frank told Tom he was pleased with how he seemed to know what he was doing and that he was glad to have him there. Tom thanked him and then vowed to himself that he would not mess this job up like he had at Morgan Manufacturing.

"I forgot to mention that I like to work at least half a day on Saturdays if we are behind like this," Frank said. "Are you willing?"

"Sure," came the reply.

"Great. See you tomorrow at eight."

On the way home, Tom decided to stop in at Pete's Place for a beer with the guys.

~~~

Marsha promised dinner and beer at the local pizzeria to bribe a couple of the guys at work to help her move. Each had a pickup truck, and since they worked on the loading dock, she knew they had the muscles for the job. George elbowed Hector and chuckled, "She wants our strong backs and weak minds."

"I did not say that, George Lindel!" she scolded with a grin. "You're just trying to start trouble." They laughed and agreed to go to the house directly after work.

Marsha was glad they were available and willing. There was no way she could lift any of the larger furniture. The larger pieces wouldn't fit in her car anyway. Besides, it would be good to have company in case Tom started something. However, he wasn't there.

"Out drinking again," she concluded. That made things easier. She even took a chest of drawers that Tom probably would have contested.

The chilly rain was not unusual for this late in the year, but at least it held off until they had all the stuff moved into the apartment. Then it was off to dinner. While she ate her salad and a slice of deluxe pizza, she marveled at her work crew's appetite. "Man, you guys can eat!" she said as they each downed a large pizza and chased it with enough beer to remind her of Tom. The bill came to more than she had expected, but the move had come off without a hitch. That made it worth the price.

~~~

Tom had promised Frank to show up on time; he didn't dare mess up. Around 8:30, he told the guys good night and headed out the door.

The tires slipped once as he pulled out of Pete's Place and again at the stop sign three blocks away. The rain had stopped, but the water had gotten cold, and the road was slick in spots.

Working on cars all day brought Glenn Abney back to mind. "I wonder how he's doing," Tom thought. "He hasn't written me since I've been home." Then he remembered he had not written Glenn either. He smiled as he thought of how weak they both were in their writing habits.

The area near Buffalo Creek is open range. It has no trees or buildings, and the wind had whipped across the road, chilling the water even faster than on the other roads. Suddenly, a gust bumped the side of the truck. Tom overcorrected, and the tires lost traction. Against all that he had been taught, fear got the best of him. Tom turned the wheel the wrong way and hit the brakes; in a split second, he spun across the highway. The back corner of the truck bounced off the guardrail catapulting it back across to the other side of the road where the front tire clipped the end of that rail, spinning him over the embankment and flipping him at the same time.

With the wheels in the air, Tom had absolutely no control. Before his heart could skip a beat, the truck was rolling down toward the creek and shaking him around like a dog abusing a rag doll.

The truck came to rest on its top in the shallow water.

~~~

On the way back to the apartment, Marsha stopped by Violet's house. Before long, they had everything in the car.

"Thanks a lot for letting me stay here, Vi."

"I am glad we could help you, Marsha. I hope everything works out all right."

"I'm sure it will," Marsha replied opening the car door. "Oh, wait," she said going around and opening the passenger side door. She moved some clothes, pulled a brown paper grocery bag off the floor, and handed it to her hostess.

"What's this?" Vi asked.

"I can't afford much, but it's a gift for you. Sorry I didn't have a chance to wrap it."

Violet got a surprised look on her face. "That's very thoughtful of you, Marsha." She opened the bag and looked inside; the surprised look gave way to a big grin. "Coooooooffeeeeeee!" she whispered with wide eyes, smiling up at Marsha.

They hugged, and Marsha left just as rain was starting to fall again.

~~~

Tom could not remember what had happened. He was sure he smelled gasoline. It reminded him of when he was a boy helping his dad pump gas into the family car.

He couldn't figure out why his arms were floating above his head and why he couldn't keep them down. And why were his hands so cold and wet? When he finally got his hands to unbuckle his seatbelt, he was further confused when he fell towards the ceiling and splashed into several inches of water. As he lay there, he began to remember what had happened and realized the truck was on its roof in the creek.

Now Tom smelled something burning. When it finally registered that he smelled burning *and* gasoline at the same time, a sense of urgency set in. The driver's side door was stuck. The passenger's side roof was caved in and the door was ajar, but it was not open enough for him to get out.

Urgency became panic! There was almost no light; he could see virtually nothing. He could feel the dashboard, so he moved himself around to kick out the windshield. His first kick did not meet the resistance that he expected as the window had broken in the rollover. He kicked again, and the window dislodged from the frame. Tom moved over to the opening and began to press his way out at the edge of the windshield.

As he emerged from under the inverted hood, he sensed that the light rain had picked up again, this time mixed with sleet. His shoulder hurt and so did his head and one of his legs. He touched his head and felt a sizable lump. Then he reached down to where his leg hurt. His eyes were starting to adjust to the dark, and when he brought his hand back up close to his face, his fingers were smeared with something dark.

Once he was out from under the truck, he could see just enough to get his bearings. He started dragging his way up to the road and got about halfway up the hill before he passed out.

~~~

Marsha pulled into the parking lot. In three trips, she had moved most of the things from the car into the apartment.

She was exhausted. She had spent half of her workday dreading a confrontation which hadn't happened. The trepidation took almost as much emotional energy as if the conflict had actually occurred. After work, she had directed and helped with the move and watched as her hires ate what seemed like half a day's pay. All of this occurred during a light rain that came and went. Now, as she moved the last of her things, the light rain was starting to mix with sleet.

A hot bath was the only thing she wanted between her and a long night in a warm bed. Soon she had taken the one and was enjoying the other.

~~~

Tom began to regain consciousness. He remembered cold and wet, but as he lay there, eyes still closed, he realized he was dry and warm. He remembered gas and burning, but the smells were different now. The noise of sleet and rain hitting his soaked suede jacket had become the soft noise of people moving around quietly, punctuated by an occasional chime. Gradually, he opened his eyes just enough to see where he was; he was in a darkened room and the only light was coming in through a door which was slightly ajar.

Just then someone came into the room. Opening the door dramatically increased the light, forcing his eyes closed again. As he began to reopen them, a woman quietly said, "Hello sleepyhead. I didn't expect to see you awake just yet."

Tom squinted to look at her. He finally recognized the nurse as Brenda Baker, one of his classmates in eleventh grade chemistry.

"What happened?" he asked through a raspy voice.

"You had an accident out on Route 38."

It took Tom a moment to process the words. "How did I get here?"

"Deputy Paulson saw pieces of metal and glass out on the bridge over Buffalo Creek and stopped to look around. It's a good thing he found you, Tom. You would have been in a lot of trouble if you had been out there much longer."

The accident was still foggy in his mind, but he was starting to recall crawling out from under the hood. "This is just great," Tom sighed. "My whole life is falling apart, and now I wreck my truck."

Brenda took his pulse and blood pressure as she continued to speak. "You should be grateful, Tom. God spared your life. You could have died."

Tom started to process that remark as she checked the IV, but before his still-cloudy mind could formulate a response, she put a thermometer in his mouth. She retrieved the clipboard from the end of the bed and jotted some notes.

The subject changed as she pulled out the thermometer and asked, "Why were you wearing a shirt with the name 'Robbie' on it?" She wrote a little more on the clipboard and then hung it back at the foot of his bed.

"I just started at Frank's Garage," he said. Then with a start, "Wait … what time is it? I have to call him and let him know I might be late." His sudden motions caused pain in several places.

"It's not quite four AM, and I'm pretty sure he has not opened yet," she said with a grin. "Besides, it's Saturday; I don't think he's open on the weekends."

"He said he was behind and asked if I could come in."

"Well, I get off duty at eight. I'll call over there before I leave and let him know what happened. Besides, I don't think you'll be going anywhere for a couple days."

With some confidence that someone was watching out for him and with the aid of the painkiller flowing through the tube in his arm, Tom drifted back to sleep.

~~~

Tom had been dreaming, but it wasn't about being in a hospital. Then he opened his eyes, saw the IV above his head, and heard noises out in the hall. Slowly, reality began to come back to him.

Brenda's words were echoing through his mind as he fell asleep, and they were among the thoughts he had as he awoke: "You should be grateful, Tom. God spared your life. You could have died."

His thoughts weren't clear, but he kept wondering about her words. "My life is such a wreck. I would be better off dead. Why didn't God just let me die? If there is a God."

The more he pondered, the more irritated he became. His reflections were interrupted when Brenda came back into the room.

"Oh, good morning, Tom. I talked to Frank, and he said to get well and come back when you can. He said he would stop by later to see how you are doing. I am about to leave and just wanted to see if you needed anything."

"Why'd he do that?" Tom snapped.

That surprised Brenda, and she wasn't sure what to say. "Well, I guess he's shorthanded and needs the help. Besides, he's a good man, Tom. He wouldn't fire you just because ..."

"No, not Frank," Tom interrupted, his anger showing. "God. Why would God spare my life? I would rather have died out in the rainy cold than keep going through this—hell, this—this hell."

"Maybe he is sparing you from a worse one, Tom. Despite all life's trials, there are worse things than what you're going through. I don't know what you're facing, but I know that nothing is so bad in this life that God can't help you through it. In fact, sometimes he uses trials in our lives for the very purpose of forcing us to depend on Him."

"I don't need God," Tom shot back, "and I don't want him either."

Brenda winced. She wasn't accustomed to words like that spewed out with so much anger, especially from someone who just hours before had kissed death on the lips. "Surely, you don't mean that," she said.

Tom laced his reply with words that made it clear that God was the farthest thing from his mind.

Brenda was not sure what to say. Finally, she opened her mouth, and what came out surprised her even more than it surprised Tom. "You have it your way, Tom Jenkins. But I can tell you this much ..." She paused. Slowly, he looked up at her expecting her wrath. Instead she stared straight into his eyes and spoke with a calm blend of strength and compassion. "You *think* you don't need God, Tom, but you're wrong."

Those words hung in the air for what seemed like forever. Tom rested his head back on the pillow and averted his gaze to the ceiling while he prepared his reply. When he finally looked back to argue with her, she was gone.

He didn't like people telling him he was wrong—about drinking, about anger, about anything. And certainly not about God!

~~~

What a day! Marsha had collapsed into bed, and her head had hardly touched the pillow before she was asleep. When she finally awoke, she went to the kitchen and started making some coffee. She grinned as she remembered Violet's animated explanation of Victor's feigned distain for her precious liquid.

She turned on the radio and tuned it to a music station. Then she sat on the couch and put her cup on the coffee table.

~~~

Brenda headed out to begin her Saturday morning after-work ritual. On the way home, she would stop for gas, pay any bills that were due, and take care of the dry cleaning if she had any. Then she would go to the store to pick up her groceries for the week. She usually didn't get home until almost 10:00 o'clock, but that way, all of her running-around chores were done for the week.

~~~

"Hi, Tom." It was Frank. "I wanted to come over and see how you are doing."

"I thought you opened the station on Saturdays."

"Well, it's not officially open. I just try to get caught up if we are behind on anything. That way I can take Saturdays off if I need to or go in afternoons if I want to do something in the mornings."

Frank asked Tom how he was doing, and they engaged in small talk for a couple minutes.

"Well, I do want to get in to the shop," Frank said. I have a carburetor to rebuild, and Debbie wants me to hang a new light fixture in the dining room this afternoon. I'll stop by again tomorrow. Is there anything you need?" Tom seemed distracted. "Tom?"

"Mmm? Oh, sorry." Tom said. Then without answering Frank's question, he asked, "Do you remember Brenda Baker from high school?"

"Yeah. She's the one who told me you were here."

"Oh, yeah."

"Why?"

"Well, she gave me a lecture about God this morning and then walked out. It makes me so mad when people act like they can read God's mind and tell me what he wants. That just drives me nuts!"

"What did she say?"

"Oh, she said that God spared my life to save me from something worse and that I need him."

He deliberately added some language he was sure would irk Brenda and was annoyed she was not there to hear his rant. "She was even religious back in high school, and she hasn't changed a bit. Where does she get off talking like that?"

Frank paused for a moment. "Well, Tom, sometimes Christians aren't exactly sure what to say, or how to say it for that matter. I'm sure she meant well. And besides, she is right about one thing—regardless of what we go through in this life, there are worse things."

"Like what?" Tom snapped. He had spent much of the morning thinking about wrecking his truck. That and his conversation with Brenda had put him a mood.

Frank sat back down in the chair. Again, he paused as if searching for words. "Look, Tom," he started. "I … I became a Christian about four months ago. I am sure of my faith; I do know that. What I don't know yet is how to explain it very well. But let me just tell you this…" Frank sighed. "You know what a bonehead I can be sometimes. I was always getting drunk, getting into fights. You know how I was pretty mean to Debbie after we got married. I don't know if I ever told you, but I cheated on her a couple times."

"No, you never mentioned that," Tom said, his mind flashing back to Linh.

"I was really making a mess of things, Tom. Then I had lunch with Billy Wilson, and he told me some stuff that the Bible says. He said God calls the stupid stuff I was doing sin. I guess I have always known that what I was doing was wrong, but then he told me something else. He said that my sins were not my main problem. My main problem is not what I do, it's who I am."

"What does that mean?" Tom asked, bristling at the words "wrong" and "sin".

"The things I do are bad, sure enough," Frank continued. "Don't get me wrong about that. It's just that I don't become a bad person because I do bad stuff. I do bad stuff because there is something wrong with me—deep down inside. No matter how hard I tried not to do what I did, it didn't change who I was. As long as I am who I am, I struggle with what I do. Does that make any sense?"

"I'm not sure," Tom replied, a little less hostile as he sensed Frank's transparent sincerity, more talking-with than preaching-at.

"I just don't think that religious stuff would work for me. I just can't be perfect like that."

"Oh, man," Frank laughed, "did I ever give you the wrong impression! I didn't mean that I'm always doing everything right or even that I have this all figured out. I'm not sure if I will *ever* get it all right; I'm just starting out on this road. But I can tell you this much: it's not just a bunch of rules—not 'thou shalts' and 'thou shalt nots' and stuff like that. There's something real about this, Tom. Something really real."

~~~

When Brenda arrived home, she parked in front of her building and got out. As she walked to the trunk to get her groceries, she saw a familiar face on the other side of the parking area.

Marsha was just getting ready to go out for some shopping of her own.

"Marsha? Marsha Jenkins?"

Marsha turned to see someone vaguely familiar.

"Hi, Marsha." Marsha's confusion was clear from her expression. "Brenda. Brenda Baker from high school." Light dawned on Marsha's face; they had not been close, but she remembered her former classmate.

Brenda continued, "What brings you into my neck of the woods?"

"You live around here?" Marsha asked.

"Yeah, Building A over there," she replied. Then she asked, "Did you see the truck? What did it look like? He was really fortunate, but he should be out in a week or two."

"Who? What truck? Out of where?" Marsha asked.

"Out of the hosp …." Brenda suddenly realized that Marsha didn't know about the accident. "O my gosh, Marsha, I thought you knew. I'm so sorry."

"Knew what?" Marsha asked, becoming irritated.

"About uh … about the accident," she answered. "Tom was banged up pretty badly, and he lay out in the rain some time before the deputy found him. He said that Tom's truck was totaled."

Brenda continued speaking, but she was saying a lot more than Marsha was hearing.

"What?" Marsha interrupted. "What … when? When did this happen? When … where is he now?"

"Last night. He's in room 312 at the hospital. I'm sorry. I figured you knew."

Marsha was already getting into her car. She started the engine, backed out, and headed toward the street.

"I'm sorry," Brenda called out again.

~~~

On the way to the hospital, Marsha wondered what she was going to say. Then she realized she wasn't even sure why she was going. After all, she was divorcing the guy. Somehow, there was a connection that she could not explain—some tie, some link that inexplicably pulled at her.

"It's the respectable thing to do," she finally concluded. "I guess I don't actually hate him anyway. I just don't want to be married to him anymore."

The drive took less time than it would have if she had obeyed the speed limits. She turned onto West Hall Road. From there, it was only three more blocks to the hospital. About a half block away, she had to pull to the side of the road to allow an ambulance to pass. She thought she might be able to beat it, but it was coming up fast enough behind her that it became apparent she would lose that race. She gave way.

Marsha was still not sure what she was going to say. The hall echoed with the click of her heels on the tile floor as if a clock were ticking away the seconds, warning her that soon she would walk through the doorway into his room. It was going to be uncomfortable enough, but the awkwardness would be compounded if she didn't have something to say. She mentally tried to string words together that would sound respectable without suggesting any commitment.

"Here it is, Room 312," she thought. She stopped to straighten her clothes, took a deep breath, and walked in.

"Hi," was all that came out of her mouth.

Tom was a little surprised to see her. Anytime in the past that their emotions had turned to face each other, Tom had felt hope. It was their last meeting at The Ranch that convinced him that he was just kidding himself, that there was no hope. Even if he did want her to stay, he was not going to hang his feelings out there where she could kick them again. Their relationship had become a tangle of faith, fears, and frayed nerves. Like a child who has learned by experience the meaning of 'hot', he impulsively started to reach out to hope but just as quickly pulled back as if he sensed danger. The Army had taught him how to face an enemy that uses bullets which pierce the skin, but he had never been trained for an enemy who had once been his friend but whose weapons ripped into the heart. He also forgot that those emotional bullets go both ways, just like real ones do.

"What happened?" she asked, cursing herself that she hadn't come up with anything more original.

"I skidded off the road," he said. Several hours of thinking was bringing back his memories of the accident.

"Were you drinking?"

"Give me a break. The road was slick." Tom's head snapped away, and he gazed out the window.

There was silence. "Same old Tom," she thought, questioning again why she had come and at the same time wishing she hadn't. Now the only thing left to do was to find a way to leave gracefully. She was glad there were no others in the room to make it even more awkward.

"I'm glad you're okay, but I found an apartment. I think we need to stop kidding ourselves."

"Yep." He was still looking away.

She stood there for uneasy moments that seemed to last forever, but Tom remained silent. She wasn't sure what that meant. She waited, thinking that there was something else to say. There wasn't. Quietly, slowly, as if immersed in thought, she finally turned and left. The sound of her heels echoed through the halls, tapping out her retreat.

She had expected more of a fight from Tom. What she had *not* expected was the trickles of warm sorrow she felt running down her face. She had decided to end their marriage; the full impact of her decision had eluded her until she realized he had given up too.

"There is nothing more I can do," she told herself. It was more an attempt at self persuasion than a statement of conviction.

~~~

"Wow, Tommy!" Glenn said as he popped his head through the doorway. "Yur messed up. You're uglier now than you ever was."

"Hey, Glenn! Well thanks a lot, buddy." They both laughed. In an instant, it was like old times.

When Tom came home, Glenn still had several months left on his tour in 'Nam, and they hadn't seen each other since. They were both bad about staying in touch; however, they had the kind of friendship in which they would tease each other mercilessly, go some time without seeing each other, and then start right back to teasing as if there had been no interruption.

"How did you know where I was?" Tom asked.

"I didn't have no good place to change my o'l, so I had Frank do it. He told me you was here. He says you's workin' for him now."

"Yeah, if you can call it that! I had my wreck on the way home after the first day. I'm not sure you can call that working for anybody." They laughed again.

"When did you get back, Glenn? I thought you were still in The Nightmare." They wrote each other several times in 'Nam, and Glenn had adopted Tom's two-word description of the place.

"I come back an' they cut me loose 'bout two months ago. I went to Or'gon to visit Liz and them for awhile and then stopped by the Grand Canyon on the way back here. That is one big hole, Tommy!"

"Yeah, I need to go there sometime. How is Liz doing?"

"Well, I could tell from her letters that she took Ma's passin' stump hard, Tommy. About a month afor I come back, she wrote me a letter wantin' I should stay with them for awhile, you know, me an' her bein' the only ones left in the family and all."

"What did Ben think about that? Didn't that get crowded?"

"Well, actual, no. Her and Ben was gettin' a little farm just 'fore you come back. They got done renovatin' the old farm house, an' they still had the trailer they was livin' in, so I just stayed there." Then he grinned with a certain mixture of pride and delight. "The kids thought it was neat having Uncle Glenn just a couple minutes away. We could just walk down to the pond and fish an' skip rocks whenever we was a mind to. I'm gonna go back next summer and take 'em swimmin'."

"Sounds like a perfect setup. What brought you back to Johnstown?"

"All my friends is here," Glenn said. Then he became reflective. He took in a breath and let it out. "Ya know, Tommy, somethin' changed Liz while we was in 'Nam. I mean she's still Sis, love her to death and all that. But after Ma died, she started going to church. I think she got a little more religion than a body needs. You know what I mean?"

"Boy, do I. Brenda Baker is a nurse here now, and she's that way. She just tried to go there with me, and I told her to leave me out of it. I don't know why people like that have to be so high and mighty."

"Well, Liz ain't so much like that," Glenn continued. "It's just … well … she just takes it so serious an' all that. I mean, I think it's fine if some folks wants to go to church and believe the Bible an' all that, but she's all the time praying an' stuff, even when she ain't in church or nothin'. An' she's forever goin' on about how God done this for her and God done that for Ben or the kids." Glenn paused. "She does seem to be more … I don't know … she ain't near as easy upset as I recollect her before."

"Well, it's all just more than I need right now," Tom said. "I have too much going on in my life at the moment. Trying to balance some god-thing on top of everything else is more of a problem than a solution."

"Yeah, I guess." After some silence, Glenn said, "Are you talkin' 'bout the accident? I mean, when you say 'everything else,' that's whatcha mean, ain't it?"

Tom began to unload his story. After a few minutes, Glenn sat down. He could tell this was going to take some time.

~~~

"It sure was good to have Glenn with us for a visit," Ben said as they sat on the porch swing watching the children play in the chill of the afternoon.

"Yeah, Honey, an' it was right good for the kids too," Liz said in her drawl. "They sure liked it when he tol' stories and took 'em fishin' an' all that."

Ben used to chuckle whenever he heard Liz and Glenn talk together because they had identical accents. Liz's voice was higher pitched, of course. She also talked faster than her younger brother, but everything else was the same.

"Yeah, both of them really got excited yesterday when I told them about the letter—that he's coming for Christmas."

"You know, Ben, I sure am glad he's back from Veet-nam." She pronounced it in two syllables like President Johnson had. "He can get about his life now."

~~~

Two weeks after she moved into the apartment, Marsha had a Friday night housewarming party in her new place. Several girlfriends from work came as did two members of her high school volleyball squad.

They tuned the radio to one of the local AM stations. It had been competing with the new FM station for the country music audience, but the manager finally decided they would go broke if they didn't change formats. He switched them to 'rock and roll' hoping that would attract young listeners who would prefer rock music to country, and it turned out to be a good move. They were really becoming adept at delivering a party sound especially on Friday nights when Jerry and Jenn bantered back and forth between cuts.

When Lucy finally arrived, she had Ray on one arm and Dalton on the other, and each of them had brought some beer. Jodi pulled Marsha into the kitchen and told her that she heard Ray often had marijuana with him whenever he went to a party.

Marsha hadn't expected the guys or their party enhancements, but it didn't take her long to warm up to the idea. "This could get interesting," she pondered. It was time to initiate this new place and she wanted to do it right!

Chapter 4 – Valleys

Glenn awoke early. It was the day he was supposed to interview for the job at Rosedale Dairy Farm. Wednesday, he had been at the hardware store looking for work, but they didn't have any openings. Mr. Burton, the foreman at Rosedale, overheard the conversation. After speaking briefly with Glenn, he said that he could use a good mechanic and asked Glenn to come out to see him on Saturday.

Well, today was Saturday, and what a beautiful day it was! The sun was shining brightly on this unusually-mild, mid-December morning. Glenn's father used to say that if we had to buy our weather, we couldn't afford days like this one.

Glenn got into his car and headed out to the Rosedale farm, a big place a couple miles east of town. He had been raised on his dad's small spread and was excited about the idea of being hired onto a larger farm. His dad's place had actually only been twenty-three acres with crops and a few hogs and chickens; they didn't have nearly the equipment that Rosedale had. "But tractors is tractors, engines is engines, and gearboxes is gearboxes," he said to himself. He was preoccupied with the prospect of a job and did not see the stop sign. Nor the semi approaching from the left.

~~~

Frank unlocked the door, turned on the lights, and took off his coat. He turned on the power switch for the inside lighting, but since it was the weekend, he left the external lights off. Then he started putting on his coveralls.

Yesterday had been a long day, the busiest since Frank bought the station going on two years ago. Today would give him the opportunity to start catching up.

It had been a couple weeks since Tom's accident, and the doctor told him late yesterday that he could go back to work. Frank was sure glad when Tom called telling him that he was finally coming back.

After buttoning up his coveralls, he went back into the bays and started working on the tune up he had left half done. Yesterday had been a *really* long day.

The bell rang as a car pulled into the station. Frank poked his head out from under the hood and saw the old clunker he had loaned

Tom until he could get another truck. "Great," Frank sighed with relief. "Things are finally going to be normal again."

Tom opened the door and walked in; Frank walked toward him with a smile.

"Welcome back, Tom," he said as he stuck out his hand. They shook hands, and Frank asked him how he felt.

"I feel great," Tom said through a huge grin. "Ready and raring to go." They talked business for a couple minutes. Frank had kept Tom informed on what was happening at the station during chitchat while visiting the hospital every couple of days. However, once Tom was back home recovering, Frank had only called him on the phone twice to see how he was doing. The conversations were shorter and had not included much small talk since work at the station was starting to backup.

This morning, they quickly covered the work list, mostly cars that had come in for repairs. Frank had been able to talk most of his customers into delaying routine work until Tom came back.

"I was tuning up the Ford in the far bay," he said. "Mrs. C let it go until it was starting to miss, so I told her we would do it right away. I just finished changing the plugs; it still needs points, condenser, and rotor. Give her a new distributor cap too," he added. "I'm not sure she needs it quite yet, so I won't charge her for it; it's just to make sure she doesn't have any trouble. Also, do an oil change and filter. I checked the oil before I took her home. Since the oil was really dark, she said to change it."

Mrs. Cavanaugh was a great third grade teacher and had taught Frank one year and Tom the next, a couple of years before she retired. Now she shared her talent by teaching Sunday School. She had become a fixture in the community. Her husband Wendell had been a mechanic in the Army before he retired. He always had taken care of their car until he passed away in February; however, Mrs. C just had driven the car until it "wasn't running right" and then brought it to Frank.

Tom started putting on his coveralls. "Hey," Frank called. "I got your new shirts in. You don't have to be Robbie anymore. They're hanging on the coat rack."

Tom took down one of the shirts and took off the plastic bag. He looked at his name on the patch sewn onto the shirt and got a sense that he actually belonged. It was such a small thing, but since he did not have anything left, belonging somewhere, anywhere, really was a big thing to him. He took off Robbie's shirt and put on his own. He looked in the mirror at his name, Tom. Actually, in the mirror it said moT and that made Tom grin. Then he pulled up the coveralls. He felt good.

He walked into the bay and started working on Mrs. C's car.

~~~

It was almost ten o'clock when Tom walked into the office where Frank was trying to catch up on the books.

"I finished Mrs. C's car," Tom said. "I thought I should give it a once over, so I found that one of the taillights was out too. I replaced it."

"Good," Frank said. "Just note the light and distributor cap as no-charges so we have a record of it." Then he added, "Thanks for thinking of that. She kinda needs a little help now that Mr. C is gone."

The phone on the desk rang, and Frank answered as Tom sat down to fill out the card. After a brief conversation, Frank finally said, "Yes sir, we'll be right out."

Frank hung up the phone and said, "You used to work over at the Esso station in Elk Point, didn't you?"

"Yeah," Tom said, "before I went into the Army."

"I bought that tow truck from them a couple of months ago when they got their new one. Do you know how to operate it?"

"I thought it looked familiar. Yeah, I took it on many-a-run in the eight months I worked there."

"Well, are you up to another run?"

"Sure. Where?"

"There was an accident where Cliff Road crosses Route 41. Go pick up the car and park it in back under the tree until they tell us what to do with it. The keys are in the cash drawer."

"Yes sir!" Tom said smiling and snapping a stiff salute. Yes, it was good to belong somewhere.

~~~

Marsha had told her mom she would come to Wellington to visit for the weekend. The party went later than she had planned, but they sure had initiated the new apartment. She took some aspirin and decided she would drive a little slower than usual until her head was clearer. The apartment was a mess, but it would be there when she got back. Fortunately, she had arranged for a day off on Monday in case she decided to spend an extra day with Mom.

There was no real reason for the visit. Well, maybe it *was* time to tell her mom that she was separated from Tom and was talking to a lawyer about a divorce.

Miss Benson was a quiet Baptist woman who made a careless choice in her late teens; she never married and raised Marsha on her own. Despite her momentary lapse, she took her faith seriously. She did not wear her convictions on her sleeve, but at the same time, she was not afraid to speak honestly about her beliefs.

Marsha knew that Mom was not going to take this news without offering advice whether Marsha asked for it or not. Her mother liked Tom and accepted him after the marriage, but when they were dating she cautioned Marsha to notice Tom's drinking and the fact that he didn't seem to take any interest in Christianity at all. However, Mom believed that once someone made a commitment they should honor it.

Marsha knew that her mother's conviction was mainly because of her Baptist teaching, but she also suspected that a certain young man had made a promise years ago on a warm summer evening and then failed to follow through. That event caused a sadness that Marsha still occasionally saw in her mother's eyes.

As she drove, Marsha mulled over how she was going to word her news. There was no good way to say it, but maybe there was a way to minimize the reaction. Besides, though she never told her mother, Christianity had never been very interesting to her either. She continued to struggle with how to tell of the pending divorce, but she did not worry about the 'religion' angle, that was something she would never tell her mom. She didn't share her mother's faith, but she did not want to hurt her either. Not any more than she had to anyway.

~~~

Tom was only a block from the station when he heard the wailing siren of an ambulance approaching from the direction of Route 41 and pulled over to the side of the road. After it passed, he started up again. Seven minutes later, he arrived at the scene of the accident.

There were two county deputies on the scene along with a firetruck. Tom carefully pulled alongside the wreckage and stopped just past what was left of a pastel yellow Corvair convertible, the car he assumed he was supposed to tow. The other vehicle was a tractor-trailer rig, and though the bumper was bent and the grill and passenger side fender were mangled, it was obvious that it was not the truck driver who had lost this fight. Besides, if the truck needed to be towed, it would take a bigger rig than Tom had.

There were pieces gathered into a pile. One officer was sweeping the remaining glass and debris off to the side of the road. The other officer was writing on a clipboard and talking to a middle-aged man who was nervously puffing on a cigarette. Tom guessed him to be the truck driver.

The fire crew was just packing up their equipment and rolling up their hoses.

Tom got out of the tow truck. As he approached the two men, he could see that the trucker was visibly shaken. "I can't …. I …. Officer, in eighteen years I have never had so much as a fender bender. Leastwise, not in my rig. I just didn't see him comin' out of that road." The officer assured him that the details of the scene were consistent with his story and that the report would show the Corvair driver to be at fault. That seemed to assure the trucker, but he was still clearly upset.

The officer turned to Tom and said that he had all the information he needed and was ready for Tom to tow the car to the shop. Then he said, "When the driver recovers, he can call you about what you should to do with the car."

"Okay," Tom said, and his mind turned toward what would not be an easy tow. This car was a mess. The truck had hit the driver's side from the front of the car back to about the middle. Since neither driver had seen the other before impact, the whole thing happened at full speed. The front half of the Corvair, including the driver's seat, had been crushed. There was blood everywhere; Tom hadn't seen this much blood since The Nightmare.

The firemen had sawed through the front roof supports and pried the roof open to get the driver out. It looked like a big open mouth, set to chomp its next victim, but this predator had claimed its last life.

Tom began the task of figuring out the best way to get this mangled mess back to the shop.

~~~

Marsha pulled off the road at a rest area. She had driven for several hours and decided it was time to stretch.

As she strolled along the path, she saw an older lady walking a small dog. It reminded her of a pet her childhood friend had, so she asked the woman what kind of dog it was.

"It's a Pekinese," she replied. "My husband bought it to keep me company when he found out he only had a couple months to live."

She went on to tell Marsha of their forty-six years together and how, even after these three years, she still missed him. "We would have been married fifty years next March," she mentioned. "I have accepted his death, but I still do miss him so, especially at night."

They talked a few more minutes and then parted ways. Marsha headed back to her car; she wanted to get to her mom's before suppertime. Mom promised to make her spectacular lasagna, and Marsha was *not* going to be late for that.

~~~

Tom slowly rolled into the station and pulled around back. Frank looked up when he heard the bell but saw it was the tow truck and went back to work on the Buick. Mr. Cranston had been down by the river to do a little fishing when he punctured the gas tank while backing over a small boulder. Frank had just made all the connections and was starting to tighten the hardware on the new tank.

After Tom maneuvered the wrecked car back into the corner under the sycamore tree, he set it down and disconnected the chains. Then he parked the truck around front and went back inside.

"Now *that* was a wreck," he called out with a certain relief that he had finished his task successfully. "It was a contest between a semi and a Corvair, and you *have* to know who lost *that* fight."

"Ouch." Frank added to the conversation, "I'll bet that wasn't pretty. I'll have to take a look when I finish this."

Tom put the truck keys back in the drawer, stepped into the service area, and got under the lift to help Frank finish up.

When they we done, they both stepped back; then Frank kicked out the stop and lowered the car to the floor. Frank emptied a gas can into the new tank and got down on his hands and knees to check for leaks. When he opened the bay door, Tom started the old Buick and backed it out to the pump to fill it up. When he was finished, he checked for leaks again, then parked it next to the tow truck and went back into the bay area. Frank was not there, but he had left the back door ajar when he stepped out to see the wreck.

"Didn't I tell ya?" Tom called as he stepped out. There was no reply. Frank was leaning against the mangled heap with both hands, his head down.

"What's the matter?" Tom asked. Frank pointed to an oil change sticker on what was left of the shattered windshield; it was from Frank's Garage. Tom had not noticed that.

"Whose car is it?" Tom asked.

"It's … it's Glenn's car," Frank finally managed to get out. "All this blood …. Did you see him?"

Tom was stunned. "Glenn Abney?" he finally asked softly. "Are you sure?" A pause and then, "No. No, he was gone when I got there."

"Did the police say anything?"

"Just that they would tell him to call us about the car."

"So he's okay?" Frank asked, looking up.

"Yeah," Tom said, starting to shake. "I mean I don't—I don't know, Frank. It was all so fast, and I didn't know—I mean the car was so …. I'm going over to the hospital to see how he is."

"Call me as soon as you know anything, Tommy," Frank called out. And then, "Never mind, I'm gonna close things up. I'll be there as soon as I can."

"Okay," Tom yelled back as he ran to the car. In moments, he was on the road driving faster than he knew he should.

Tom's mind began to turn over all the possibilities. "That just couldn't be Glenn's car. But the sticker—maybe someone else was driving it. Or maybe he broke down and a friend gave him a ride home and the car was empty when the truck hit it. Yeah, that was it. No, wait—the blood. And the truck driver said the car ran out in front of him. Okay. Okay, yeah, he loaned it out, and someone else was driving. That was it."

Tom's mind twisted and turned with every new thought, with every new possibility. Glenn was okay though; he *knew* that much.

~~~

After the longest thirty-five minutes in Tom's life, the doctor came into the waiting room. It was Doctor Johns who had removed Marsha's appendix on the Christmas Eve after they got married. His scrubs were splattered with blood. When he found out that Tom was the one awaiting news of Glenn, he started over to him. The look on his face got to Tom before the words did. "I am sorry, Tom," he said.

"There was too much internal injury. There was just nothing we could do. Glenn is gone. I'm sorry. "

Tom collapsed into the chair and began to weep uncontrollably. Dr. Johns put his hand on Tom's shoulder, but Tom was inconsolable. After a few moments, the doctor repeated his regrets. He was not sure what Tom heard, but he had to return to surgery.

As the doctor left, he walked passed Brenda Baker. She normally worked third shift but was working today to cover for a friend.

Brenda had paused in the doorway, watched as the doctor spoke to Tom, and had seen Tom break down. Earlier, she had been in the ER entrance when they brought Glenn in. She almost didn't recognize him and had listened in horror as the paramedics described the accident scene. The early prognosis was not good; she could tell from what she had just seen that Glenn had lost his final battle.

She had no idea what to say to Tom. Following their initial blowup after Tom's accident, his response to her inquires had been guarded and strictly about the business at hand:

"How do you feel?"

"I'm fine."

"Are you finished with your lunch?"

"Yes."

"Can I get you anything?"

"No, I am okay for now."

For the remainder of his hospital stay, he never made eye contact with her again.

Brenda hesitated for a few more moments while Tom's sobbing softened to quiet weeping. Slowly, she walked over and stood there searching for words.

"I am so ..." she started to say but was interrupted in mid-sentence when he suddenly jumped up and embraced her tightly. He buried his head on her shoulder and began to sob again. It was as if she represented everything in his life that was dissolving before his eyes, and he was afraid that if he let her go, it would all be gone.

His grip hurt her, but she didn't resist. She could tell that what was gripping him hurt more.

"I don't know ... what ... what I'm ... what I'm going to do, Brenda," he said between sobs. He had started out as a tough guy even before he went to 'Nam; now here he was, reduced to melted confusion.

"I know," she responded softly, unsure of what more to say.

He began to regain his composure and slowly released her.

"I'm sorry, Brenda," he managed to get out.

"I understand. I know you and Glenn were good friends. It hurts a lot when you lose someone you're close to." Her mind flashed to the unintended double meaning of her words. In the days that followed Tom's accident, Brenda found out that Marsha's move to her complex was a part of her leaving Tom. This must be terribly hard on him to suffer the loss of two people at the same time. She knew nothing of Linh.

~~~

The sun was setting, and the evening chill was becoming cold. Liz said, "Honey, I really don't like the kids out this late of an evening."

"I know, Liz. This is probably the last time this year they can be out this late. I am glad for the warmer weather we have had these last several days, but I think Old Man Winter is starting to settle in for a long stay."

Ben called the children in and helped them off with their coats. "Now you kids go on upstairs and get into your pajamas. Then come back down, and I'll read you a story."

"Okay, Daddy!" they said together, racing toward the steps of the remodeled farmhouse. Melissa was always first to the top with her long, slender legs, while the younger 'Little Glenn' had to navigate one step at a time holding on to the spindles of the handrail. He was proud that he had learned to hold on, thus earning his parents permission to traverse the steps by himself.

Ben picked up the mail Liz had brought in earlier and sat down at his desk to review the bills while the kids got ready for bed. He knew full well that he would have to take Little Glenn's top off and turn it around, but he liked the children doing as much for themselves as they knew how.

The doorbell rang.

"Ya 'specting somebody?" Liz called from the kitchen.

"No, Honey," Ben called back. "I'll get it."

He walked into the hall and reached for the door. Both surprise and reluctant interest were clear on his face when he opened it and found a state trooper on the porch.

"Hello, I'm Officer Bellings," he announced. "May I come in?"

It took a moment for the words to sink in. "Sure. Sure," Ben said as he stepped back and drew the door open.

"Who is it?" Liz asked as she walked into the hallway, wiping her hands on a dishtowel.

"Honey, this is Officer Bellings."

"Pleased to meetcha," she said as she walked up next to Ben. There was an awkward moment, and then the trooper asked, "Are you Elizabeth Webster?"

Liz looked quizzically at Ben, then back to Bellings. "Yes, sir."

"Do you have a brother named Glenn Abney?"

Ben sensed Liz starting to weaken; he put his arm around her and braced himself. This was not going to go well.

~~~

After they broke the news to Melissa and Little Glenn, the kids cried themselves to sleep. Ben carried them up to bed but woke them up in the process. The grief-stricken couple had to sit with the grief-stricken children until their little sobs carried them back into the Land of Nod.

Liz and Ben then moved quietly into their own room and continued the mourning where the little ones had left off. They grieved, cried, and reminisced late into the night, recalling their fears for Glenn while he was in Vietnam and puzzling at the cruel irony of his death here at home so soon after his return. Bits and pieces of the conversation would turn to the arrangements that they knew they must start making in the morning.

Liz recalled the many times during his visit that she looked out the kitchen window and saw Glenn sitting on a knoll overlooking their pond. Liz was sure he would like that as his resting place. Ben agreed, but they concluded that the funeral should be in Johnstown since all of Glenn's friends were there.

They called Pastor Bob to tell him what had happened and that they would not be at church in the morning. Bob called his seminary roommate Wayne Hamilton who had a small church on the outskirts of Johnstown. Wayne agreed to pick Liz up at the airport and have the memorial service at his church. He mentioned that his son and daughter were both staying at the college for some ministry planning and wouldn't be home until Christmas Eve, so Liz and the family could stay with them.

More tears. A couple more phone calls. More grieving. More memories. Finally, mercifully, sleep.

The morning broke on broken hearts.

Morning was usually a special time for the Websters with happy laughter and a good breakfast. Ben cooked the eggs and bacon or sausage while Liz got the children up and dressed. It was a family joke that Ben often burned the first pieces of toast. "We really need to get a new toaster," he'd chuckle. He would just scrape the burned pieces and put them on his plate; then he'd turn the dial back a little further and start another batch.

This morning was different. It could be spelled m-o-u-r-n-i-n-g. Liz recalled the passing of her mother last year, compounding her sorrow. One of Melissa's tears got into her mouth. "Mommy, it tastes like salt." It was the first time she had noticed that. It was not the first time she had cried, but tears did not flow often in the Webster house. They didn't need to. Ben and Liz had a good home where laughter and joys far outnumbered sorrows, much like the two homes in which they were raised. Today was one of the rare occasions where the clouds of sadness smothered the sparkle of life. Almost any other day, laughter rang throughout their home; this morning, sorrow, like a pungent odor, permeated the very air they breathed.

As they ate breakfast, Ben mentioned the time that Uncle Glenn had taken the kids into town for ice cream and told the kids to lick around the edges so it didn't drip on their clothes but then spilled his own milkshake all down the front of his shirt. Everyone smiled and Melissa laughed out loud. He brought up a few other memories, some about Glenn, some of other things, causing a chuckle here and a giggle there. It was not enough to disrupt the solemnity of the moment; it was just enough to allow sorrow to visit while keeping despair at bay.

They finished breakfast. Ben cleared the table, and then kept the children busy while Liz packed the suitcases. Blurred eyes made the task harder than she had expected. She wiped her eyes and quietly sobbed a prayer for strength.

~~~

"We'll get there as quickly as we can," Ben told her. Arrangements had to be made, but flying all four of them to Johnstown and back was simply not in the family budget. Liz would fly; Ben and the kids would follow her in the car arriving Tuesday afternoon. When Ben called the funeral home that morning, the director said that he could accommodate a Wednesday service and then arrange for the body to be sent back to Oregon.

At the airport, Liz kissed and hugged Melissa and little Glenn. She melted into tears as she embraced Ben. Then she hugged the children once more, walked over to the passenger stairs, and started to climb. At the top, she turned to wave to her family and then disappeared into the plane.

~~~

Tom awoke with a start. The nightmare he was having about *The Nightmare* had scared him awake, but as he gained his awareness, he realized that things weren't any better awake. His best friend was gone. It didn't really make any difference whether it was a bullet in 'Nam or an accident in Johnstown, Glenn was gone. He was gone. The word *gone* washed over him in a torrent.

Suddenly he realized that he was not helping himself with that line of thinking. "I've got to just make it through the funeral," Tom said aloud. "Then I can figure out what I am going to do." The thought of the gun crossed his mind, but he had not gotten to that point — not yet anyway.

Glenn was gone, and Marsha was gone, and Linh was gone. At least he still had some hope with the job. Frank had been good to him. He especially appreciated that Frank had not hammered him with his religion. He had been open and honest in their discussions but had not tried to force Tom to believe anything.

He thought of Glenn's Corvair that he had towed back to the garage. He felt compelled to go look at it again now that it was more than just the bent metal and broken glass it had been when he first saw it. Frank didn't open the station on Sundays, but the Corvair was out back. He was just going to stop by for a minute.

It suddenly seemed strange to him that he had not recognized Glenn's car. Then he realized he had never seen him in it. Glenn had a light green Rambler before he went into the service; that was the car which always came to mind whenever Tom thought of Glenn. In the several weeks since Glenn came back, Tom had never seen him in the Corvair. Tom concluded that he must have bought it out West after he was discharged.

Reluctantly, he got up and started to dress.

"Hi, Liz, I am Pastor Wayne. This is my wife Betty."

"Hi, back," Liz said in her drawl. Wayne and Betty later mused at her cute accent. Her bubbly personality quickly endeared her to Betty especially knowing the tragedy that had just struck Liz.

"How was your flight?" Betty asked.

"It was real bumpy, and I was scared half to death," Liz said. "This is the first time I ever was in an air-a-plane."

"Well, we are glad you got here safely," Betty assured her.

Wayne drove while Betty sat in the back with Liz so they could talk. Even with her upbeat attitude, there were times Liz would choke up and turn her head away. Betty had recently lost a brother to a heart attack, so she knew something of Liz's heartache.

~~~

Marsha was right. Her mom did indeed offer unsolicited advice, and just as Marsha had determined to do, she endured her mother's homily quietly. The weekend began with its share of friction, but eventually Miss Benson urged Marsha to think carefully about what she was doing and said she would pray for her. In return, Marsha said that she would think carefully and that she appreciated the prayers. Soon the subject of divorce evaporated from the conversation.

The rest of the weekend went well. They shopped, ate out several times, and went to see a play the local theater club was putting on. Since things had turned out reasonably well, Marsha stayed Sunday night and then left just after breakfast on Monday. The remainder of the day would be split between driving home and reversing the damage caused by initiating her apartment.

"Now *that* is how you throw a party!" she said out loud as she drove. The party was another thing that she had not discussed with her mother.

~~~

Just as they planned, Ben and the kids arrived Tuesday afternoon. It had been a long drive, but the only casualty was one of the front tires which picked up a nail.

While Ben and the children were on the road, Liz had finalized the plans with the funeral director. Then, she spent some time going over the service with Pastor Wayne. She gave him a list of songs she wanted sung and said she would like to say a few things during the service.

She also spent some time becoming friends with her hostess. Betty finally mentioned losing her brother. Having gone through a similar experience created a bond of which folks outside that camp knew little.

"What did ya do?" she asked. "I mean, I know that ya have to trust in the Lord and all, but what do ya do to stop the hurtin'? When Ma died, I didn't know Jesus. It hurt somethin' fierce. Same when Pa died. It does seem to be a little better this time, but it still hurts like lightnin' hittin' an ol' tree stump."

"Just wait," Betty said. "That is the only thing that I know to tell you." Then she added, "Except for trusting the Lord, but you already mentioned that. I am sure that losing your mother and father before you had the Lord to lean on made it harder, but even now, with Him near to us, losing loved ones takes time to accept. God knows what He is doing, but often we do not. It takes us some time to adjust to what He is working out in our lives."

"Yep, I know that for sure. I wuz just wondering if there was a short path around some of it. I guess not, an' that's okay as long as I know God's with me."

Betty smiled as tears filled her eyes. "Your young faith encourages me, Elizabeth." Their connection was close. To Betty, it was like having another daughter she just met.

~~~

"Hello."

"Hi, Marsha. This is Helen." Helen Brokaw was one of the volleyball friends who had been over for the apartment initiation.

"Oh, hi."

"Did you hear about Glenn Abney?"

"No, what about him?"

Helen went on to tell of the accident. Helen's older sister was dating one of the officers who had been on the scene, so she had the 'inside scoop'. She liked the feeling of knowing something that others didn't, at least not until she told them.

"The funeral's tomorrow. Are you coming?"

"Probably not. I am sure Tom will be there, and I just don't need that right now."

"Okay," Helen said, adding that she would call Marsha and tell her all about the funeral. Marsha was not enamored with that prospect but didn't say anything.

They chatted about the party for a few minutes. Then Helen said she had to make a couple more calls, and they hung up.

Chapter 5 – Streams

Tom sat on the edge of the bed. He had not slept well since Glenn's death.

The phone had awakened him five minutes earlier. Frank asked him if he was okay and if he wanted them to pick him up on the way to the memorial service.

"No. I'll be all right," he said. Even as they spoke, Tom wondered if that was the right choice. This was not going to be an easy day. It might be a good thing to ride with friends. Still, he said nothing further about it. Before they hung up, Frank said for Tom to call him if he changed his mind. Tom assured him he would.

He stumbled to the bathroom and began to get ready. He looked into the mirror and wondered about life. "What is it for? Why do things like this happen? This is not fair. Shouldn't someone make things fair?"

Over and over in his mind came thoughts of fairness, of right, of good, of sense. This whole thing just didn't make sense. Nothing in his whole life made any sense. He struggled to keep his mind focused on getting ready.

~~~

The memorial service was held at the church where Wayne was pastor. They had a small building on the outskirts of town. Tom pulled in and parked in the front corner of the lot away from the building.

He sat there thinking for what seemed like a long time. A jarful of butterflies suddenly escaped into his stomach. Even knowing what he must do, his mind kept hoping to delay the inevitable by waiting. Several more cars pulled in. After a few minutes, he got out of the car and made his way across the parking lot.

As he went inside, he realized that it had been a long time since he had been in a church building. One of his foster mothers had taken him to Sunday School when he was four years old, but the next year he was adopted. Marion and Lindsay Jenkins were pretty good people, and they didn't feel like they needed religion. Later, he had gone to Miss Benson's church on Easter Sunday when he was dating Marsha. Of course, he was in church for their wedding and again in

December for the Christmas play. The next spring, he left for The Nightmare. He had not been to church since he came back home.

Tom's eyes were drawn to the front of the sanctuary. The severity of the accident had made a closed casket necessary. His mind flashed back to the scene he had witnessed out on Route 41. He was torn between not being able to see his friend one last time and the apprehension of what that last glimpse might look like.

Ben and Liz were standing beside the casket, speaking to another couple. Off to one side, the two children sat quietly, looking at a book.

He felt like a fish out of water and began to look around for someone he knew. He saw Frank and Debbie talking to a man. Tom later found out that the man was their pastor Wayne Hamilton. Debbie's face was red around her eyes, and she kept touching them with her handkerchief. Suddenly, the reality of the whole thing pressed in on him and made him feel very helpless.

As he stood there with his thoughts, Frank excused himself and came over to greet him. Debbie finished a few words with Wayne and then joined her husband. About that time, the organ started to play and people began to find their seats.

After a few hymns, Liz got up and walked over to a microphone. In a familiar accent that first surprised and then pleased Tom, she began to speak about her brother. She only got out a few sentences before she began to weep. Ben went up to help. As he arrived, she said something softly. Ben nodded in Wayne's direction as he helped her back to her seat.

Another hymn, then someone read something. Tom was sure he had heard it before—something about a shepherd, a rod and staff, and then something about walking through a valley of shadows. "The valley of shadows," Tom thought to himself. "If there ever were words that describe *my* life ...."

"Family and friends," Wayne started, "we gather today to remember and mourn our loss of Glenn Abney, brother to Elizabeth Webster, brother-in-law to Benjamin, uncle to Melissa and young Glenn, and friend to many of you sitting here." Wayne continued to comfort those gathered. He even raised tearful laughter with a couple of the funny stories about Glenn which he had drawn from his conversations with Liz and Ben.

After a little bit, he paused and seemed to be reflecting before he went on. "Elizabeth has asked me to share something with you as we close our memorial to Glenn, something she had talked over with

Glenn during his recent visit with them. Some of you know that Glenn and Elizabeth's father passed away several years ago, and then their mother died last year. After Mrs. Abney's passing, Elizabeth felt that she really needed to search out answers about life, and death, and meaning. Eventually, she came to a place of confidence and faith in Jesus Christ. She asked me to briefly share that story with you the same way that she shared it with Glenn."

Wayne went on to explain that our sins separated us from God, but in his tender mercy, God allowed his Son Jesus Christ to pay for our sins by dying on the cross. His burial was the confirmation of his death. "But that is not all," Wayne continued. "The gospel also includes the resurrection which is the evidence that God the Father was satisfied with the sacrifice of Christ as payment for our sins. When the Lord appeared to the people after his resurrection, God was giving them proof that Jesus had solved the sin problem forever."

Tom was uneasy at first, but soon he was intrigued as Wayne spoke. It was the first time he had ever heard anyone explain God's love for people. Oh, he had heard people say, "God loves you", but this was the first time he remembered someone actually explaining it. Moreover, it was coming from a man who didn't seem to condemn him or act like he was better than him.

When he was finished speaking, Wayne prayed, and then the organist played a hymn. Tom did not recognize the piece but he noticed that even though no one asked them to, many of the people were singing the words to themselves, softly, almost as if it were a prayer set to music.

When the organ stopped playing, Wayne stepped up again and announced that Glenn's body would be buried in Oregon, so there would be no gravesite gathering. "However, the church has prepared a luncheon, and all are welcome to move to the fellowship hall in the basement for a meal and time together." People talked briefly and then slowly began to move in the direction of the pleasant aromas.

Tom was still thinking about the pastor's message, so he asked if he could sit with him as they ate. Wayne had noticed Tom's interest during the service and assured him that he would like that. By the time they sat down, most of the folks had commented to Wayne about the service, so the two of them were mostly uninterrupted as Tom began to ask his questions. "Tell me again about that gospel thing. How did Jesus fix anything by dying? How could Jesus come back to life if he died?" None of the questions were posed as trick questions; Tom really didn't understand.

Wayne perceived that and answered Tom's questions in general conversation, but when they finished eating, he suggested they continue their conversation upstairs in his study where it would be quieter. Tom agreed, and soon they were in the office where Wayne motioned to a chair and encouraged Tom to have a seat. Wayne went around and sat behind his desk.

As he sat down, Tom suddenly realized where he was. The butterflies returned to his stomach. Wayne continued the conversation, and soon Tom was at his comfort level again.

As they spoke, Tom mentioned again that he didn't quite understand what Wayne had said. "I've never had anyone explain that stuff to me like that. I thought I was starting to understand it, but it got all jumbled up again."

"That is understandable, Tom," Wayne said. "The gospel is a very simple message, but it is also the most amazing message any of us will ever hear. Sometimes the mind does a double take at the astonishing simplicity of the gospel."

"But why did Jesus die? You talked like that was a good thing, but if Jesus was good why do you think that it was a good thing for him to die?"

"That's a very good question, Tom," Wayne replied. "Think of it this way. Frank says you work for him. Well, suppose that you owned your own garage and had a very expensive collection of tools and equipment."

"I wish," Tom said with a chuckle.

Wayne grinned at Tom's comment. "It would be nice, huh?"

"Yeah."

"Well, how would it make you feel to come in to work one morning to find your door open and all of your tools and equipment gone? Just stolen. How would that make you feel?"

Wayne looked at Tom and waited for a reply. "It would make me mad as hell!" Tom said. "Uh, I mean, it would make me mad. Sorry."

"Sure," Wayne said. "And you would be right to be angry wouldn't you? Someone comes into your shop and steals your things. Not only has he broken in where he doesn't belong, but he has taken the tools and equipment you have worked so hard to buy."

Wayne paused a moment and then continued, "Now suppose the thief calls you and apologizes? Suppose he wants you to forgive him. What do you say?"

"I wouldn't do it," Tom snapped. "He doesn't deserve it."

"Right. You're right. He doesn't deserve it," Wayne said. "You're exactly right. He doesn't deserve to be forgiven." Another pause. He could see Tom thinking, so he continued to wait.

After a bit, Tom broke the silence. "But …. But I thought Christians had to forgive."

"Well, yes," Wayne said. "We are supposed to forgive. You're right about that. But let's take this one step further. Suppose you changed your mind. Suppose you decided to forgive him, but you want him to bring your tools back. Just suppose that he couldn't because he had sold all of them and spent all the money; nevertheless, he still wants you to forgive him. Now what do you say?"

"I'd nail his—his—uh, I'd—I'd nail him to the wall."

"And your anger would be right, wouldn't it?"

Tom thought about how unchristian that must have sounded, and with a certain shame in his voice, he replied, "No, I guess not."

"Are you sure?" Wayne responded. "Think about it for a minute. The person has done something wrong. We are not supposed to be unkind, and we are not to seek our own revenge on the guy. However, being angry at wrongdoing is not only acceptable, it is the only proper response."

After another moment of silence, Tom said, "Yeah. Yeah, I can see that."

"All right, now suppose that you decide that he was wrong, that you are angry with him, and that he doesn't deserve to be forgiven. Let's also suppose you decide to forgive him anyway. If he can't pay you back or replace your stuff, then who is going to suffer the loss?"

Tom thought for a moment and then suggested, "Me?"

"Exactly. If there is going to be peace between you and the thief, you will have to suffer the loss. Whether you actually go out and pay for new equipment or not, in order for there to be peace, you will have to accept the loss of what he stole."

"I understand."

"Okay, now you know a little of how it is with God. We made him angry—*rightfully* angry—because we have disobeyed him and have rebelled against him. We've done things our own way. Basically we have told God by our actions that he doesn't know what is best for us and that we know better than he does. That is an insult to God, Tom. When we do what we want to do instead of what God tells us to do, he calls that sin."

"Yeah, Frank was telling me about that," Tom commented, his mind going back to the conversation in the hospital.

"And that is not just you, Tom, that is all of us. Every one of us came into this world the same way."

Wayne picked up the Bible on his desk, then came around and sat down in the chair next to Tom. He opened the Bible, flipped several pages, and then turned the book in Tom's direction pointing to a sentence that was underlined in pen. "Please read this verse, Tom."

"For all have sinned, and come short of the glory of God." Silence. Finally, Tom spoke, "I never liked to think about it, but I know that it's true." He looked up at Wayne. "For me, I mean."

"Actually, for all of us, Tom. Not just you. All of us have sinned." He let that sink in for a moment. Then he continued, "Now, the difference is that you can choose not to replace the stolen tools; you can just close your shop. However, God cannot do that. If I can say this reverently, Tom, in the spiritual world all the books have to balance, so to speak. It is against God's character, against his very nature, for things to be out of balance. That is the bad news. The *really* bad news is that death is the penalty for sin."

Tom flinched, and his face filled with apprehension. "Death?"

"Yes." Wayne turned the page and pointed to another underlined verse. "This is what God says just three chapters later in Romans, chapter six."

Tom read, "For the wages of sin is death, but the gift of God is eternal life through Jesus Christ our Lord." Tom shuttered.

Wayne said, "This verse tells us that the wages, the paycheck, what I earn for my sin, is death. Tom, I deserve death. Just like your thief, I do not deserve to be forgiven. The other verse back in chapter three tells us that this penalty applies to *all* of us."

"But don't we all die? What is Hell? People talk about Hell. Is that for real?"

"Good questions, Tom. The death that verse is speaking about is not just when this life ends; it is what the Bible calls the second death. Physical death is when the spirit is separated from the body. The second death is when everything about a person is completely separated from any sense of the redeeming presence of God. No grace, no mercy, no love, no hope. What is left is God's righteous wrath against our sins."

Wayne continued, "You see, Tom, we are sensitive to beauty and uplifting things. We think of that as spirituality. We enjoy a spectacular sunset or hear an uplifting piece of music and refer to that as a spiritual experience. Those things work in us at the level of our souls, our minds, and our emotions. Sometimes we use the words soul and spirit interchangeably; however, our spirit works on an entirely different plane than our emotions. The spirit is the part of us that works on the 'God level'."

Wayne paused again to let Tom absorb what he was saying. Shortly, Tom said, "Okay, that verse says that we are supposed to die because of our sins, but isn't there some way that—I mean, it says 'the gift of God'—what is the gift of God?"

Wayne pointed to the verse, and Tom read again: "For the wages of sin is death, but the gift of God is eternal life through Jesus Christ our Lord."

"Death and life at the same time?" Tom puzzled, almost to himself.

"Do you remember your first question? Why did Jesus have to die?"

"Yes."

"And you remember that everything has to balance—all accounts have to be settled?"

"Yeah."

"How are you going to deal with that death penalty, Tom?"

Tom thought for what seemed like an eternity. Then he looked at Wayne. His answer escaped his lips in a terrified whisper, "I don't know."

"That is why Jesus chose to die, Tom. It is as if I were standing in front of a firing squad, and just as the trigger is pulled, someone steps in front of me and takes the bullet that I deserve. Jesus, God in the flesh, willingly took the wrath that we deserve for our sins. The penalty was paid, the books all balance, so God's anger—His righteous wrath, that we *both* admit we deserve—was satisfied without God having to banish us to that awful place, Hell."

Tom thought long on those words. He had seen a firing squad once, and it was not on his list of things he wanted to do again. Ever! He had never spent a lot of time thinking about God's anger against sin, but Tom knew the secrets of his own heart. He was sure that if God had *any* sensitivity toward wrongdoing, he was in a whole lot of trouble!

While he was pondering, Wayne turned to another verse. "Paul wrote two letters to the church in a city named Corinth. Read what he wrote in chapter five of the second letter."

Tom read verse 21 aloud, "For he hath made him to be sin for us, who knew no sin; that we might be made the righteousness of God in him."

Wayne continued, "Someone called that 'the great exchange': God took my sin, put it on Jesus Christ, and punished him for it; now God can take Christ's righteousness and put it on me. God can credit it to my account."

"But that's not fair," Tom protested with tears in his eyes. He was beginning to see the enormity of his own guilt. Though Tom longed to be forgiven, he knew that he had no right to ask God to punish the innocent for the guilty.

"Tom, no one made Jesus do that; he loved us and willingly died for us. God poured out his wrath against our sin on Christ. Once that price was paid, God declared that those who put their faith in him are righteous; that in his eyes, we are no longer guilty of those things we have done. It is not that God is just playing word games; it is that the High Court of Heaven has tried our case, and we have been found innocent because there is no unpaid balance. Jesus paid our sin debt!"

By this time, Tom was sobbing. 'Mr. Tough Guy' was again reduced to tears. However, this time it was not because his life was a wreck; it was because he finally saw that there was hope! "What do I have to do to get that—to be forgiven," he managed to get out.

"Well, in the third chapter of the gospel of John another guy was asking the same kinds of questions. Jesus told him, 'For God so loved the world that he gave his only begotten Son, that whosoever believeth in him should not perish, but have everlasting life.' That old fashion word 'believeth' has the same meaning as having faith or trust. The Bible says that without faith it is impossible to please God. How that faith works is that you go to God and admit that he is right, and admit that you cannot do what it takes to pay for your sins. Ask God instead to forgive you because Jesus has already paid the sin debt. God forgives all who come to him with repentant and trusting hearts. Believe him that he has done it because God cannot lie; he will forgive you."

Tom listened intently and then asked, "But what do I—what do I say?"

"There are no magic words, Tom; the real key is not to be phony. God already knows everything about us, so be honest with him. Don't try to hide anything; just tell him why you are coming to him. Admit that you realize you have been wrong and you cannot undo that, but that you're sorry and you trust him to use Jesus' sacrifice to pay for your sins. Tell God that you want him to help you change into the person he wants you to be."

Tom still seemed unsure so Wayne continued. "I'll tell you what. Why don't I pray briefly? Then you talk to God in your own words. Just be honest with Him."

They bowed their heads. Wayne thanked God for his grace and for sending Jesus, his only begotten Son, to pay their great sin debt. Then, he asked the Lord to hear Tom's prayer.

When Wayne finished, Tom began to realize that he was about to actually talk to God, the very God whom he had offended, rejected, and cursed all his life. He became overwhelmed at the thought and began to weep, "God, I am so sorry. God, I am so sorry. I am so sorry. God, I have sinned and done all those things you know about." Then he began to list one thing after another, and his heart just broke before God. He prayed for several minutes as things came to his mind—big things, little things, things he was not sure were even sins, but things he thought seemed to be wrong. Finally, he stopped, not because he had exhausted his list, but because his recollection of his sins had exhausted him. In his weakness, he continued to pray silently as the thoughts came.

In time, Tom raised his head. He looked at Wayne and slowly began to realize that he had a sense of peace that he had never known in *all* of his life. The burden of years of self-centeredness, rebellion, and deceit had been replaced with an overwhelming awareness that God loved him and forgave him—that Jesus had actually paid the penalty for his sins and that he was *forgiven!* It wasn't until later that Tom would discover verse 6 in Isaiah, chapter 53, which says, "All we like sheep have gone astray; we have turned every one to his own way; and the LORD hath laid on him the iniquity of us all."

Tom and Wayne continued to talk. They both lamented not knowing Glenn's final decision about what Liz had shared with him, but they rejoiced greatly in Tom's newfound faith.

After a time, Wayne suggested that Tom come over to his house next door. Liz and the family were staying one more night, and Tom could meet them and stay for supper.

"I'd like that," Tom said. "I'd like that a lot!"

Epilogue 1

That evening, Tom became fast friends with Liz and Ben. The children quickly accepted him as their 'other uncle' when Ben explained that he was Uncle Glenn's friend. Ben told him that they had decided to keep the trailer for whenever his parents or others came to visit. They invited Tom to come out sometime, and he promised he would.

Tom started going to Wayne's church, and they too became good friends. They met for breakfast every Monday and discussed the Bible, life, and fishing, although not always in that order. Tom also started going with Frank to Wayne's Wednesday night Bible study.

As his new life began to unfold, Tom learned that the Christian life is not a simple list of do's and don'ts. It is a relationship between God and one of his children. He also found out that the Christian life was not always simple at all. He remembered telling Frank, "I just can't be perfect like that." His unfolding life regularly reminded him of just how true those words were. He still had struggles with many aspects of his life including his temper and his quick tongue. But as weeks and months passed by, he found those weaknesses began to lessen as he yielded his will to God.

Wayne explained, "The word 'LORD' has a similar flavor to the word 'boss'. Jesus is Lord whether we yield to him or not, but it is when we recognize that fact and obey him that his Lordship becomes meaningful to us personally."

Tom also learned that God answers prayer, but that sometimes the answer is different from what we ask. Marsha went through with the divorce and later moved to South Carolina. Tom was particularly disappointed in that turn of events because he thought that the changes in his life were things that Marsha would like. The hope that he had lost for his marriage had budded, only to wither once again before his disappointed eyes. "I know God knows what He is doing," he told Wayne. "It's just that *I* don't know what God is doing. It's hard to give up that part of my life."

Wayne assured him that even if Marsha wouldn't be his friend, God would be his friend and pointed him to Proverbs 18:24: "There is a friend that sticketh closer than a brother." Tom found that truth added a great strength in his life.

Tom wrote Alice Benson, Marsha's mother, and told her of his new faith. She called him long distance after she read the letter and was just as excited as he was. They talked for over an hour. During the years, they continued their correspondence, sprinkled with occasional phone calls. Tom would often drive a little out of the way to visit with her on his way out to see Liz and Ben.

The Websters grew in their faith too. They mourned their loss but continued their walk with God. They especially looked forward to Tom's visits and would talk about what Glenn had meant to them. Tom helped Liz by filling in some of the gaps in what her brother had written from Vietnam. They also encouraged each other in the Lord and were excited to show each other some new gem they had just found in the Bible. And the children? Well, they really liked it when their new uncle came to visit and took them out to the pond to go fishing or swimming.

Ten months later, Liz and Ben also added one more precious member to their little family. It was another girl. They named her Tommie.

Part 2

Chapter 6 – The Day of Night

To quote Dickens, "It was the best of times, it was the worst of times" but with one exception: it was *not* the best of times.

This April afternoon was just like any other. Well, almost like any other except that today Paul sat on a different park bench. The joy of life was now only an echo somewhere in the back of his heart.

His frame slumped motionless, but his mind slogged through the past hours. And days. And months. All that surrounded him was as it usually was—children played and jumped and ran. Their parents sat on other benches or blankets or the green grass. They talked and laughed. Several kids watched as their father launched a kite and fed it string until it became a small, red diamond against the deep blue canopy of space overhead.

The spring chill in the air was advancing now. If it had another few hours of daylight, the sun would have gotten the temperature a little more comfortable. However, Sol had almost finished his course for the day. His jog across the sky was almost at an end; he would have to try to warm the earth again tomorrow.

Paul looked at his watch; it was 5:35 PM. He had been sitting there almost four hours. He was cold. It slowly dawned on him that he had been cold for a time, perhaps even since he came to the park. He noticed he had no jacket; he must have left it at the hospital.

Finally, the chill convinced him that it was time to do what he knew he eventually must do; it was time to go home. The thought left him weak. Paul rose to leave. His legs hurt. His chest hurt. His head hurt. His heart hurt.

Park Avenue ran along the southern edge of Brickle Park. He walked across the street with his head cast down and then started the two-block trek up Corban Street. As he walked, his eyes began to melt into warm, stinging pools.

He approached his house just as his next-door neighbor was leaving hers. Mrs. Connelly had worked at the hospital almost thirty years now. She received the bad news when the hospital called asking her to come in after one of the other nurses went home sick. As she reached her car at the curb, she saw him coming up the sidewalk.

"Paul, I am so sorry to hear about Barbara. She was a lovely girl." Paul failed to look up but mumbled something that sounded like, "Thank you". The words were forced through a throat that was choking with grief, so it was not as clear as it otherwise might have been. She understood.

This was the first night that he would spend without Barbara. The last several nights, when she finally became too weak to be at home, he had slept in a chair in her hospital room. They had hardly spent a night apart since they married, four years ago in June.

He made his way to the door, went in, and lay down. Within moments, the couch became a river of tears. Exhausted, peace finally came into that lonely, broken place. He would not stir again until morning.

~~~

Shortly after Barbara slept her way into the life beyond, Nurse Rhonda Baker called her husband Mike. They had been high school friends with Paul and Barbara. In fact, Paul dated Rhonda while Mike dated Barbara; however, the four of them soon recognized the mismatch and rearranged their relationships, remaining good friends. The four of them had gone to Wilson Community College over in Matson. "The Four Amigos" they had called themselves. After graduation, they celebrated with a double wedding. No one in Wellington could remember another double wedding in the town's eighty-eight-year history.

Mike had been at the hospital just that morning but had gotten a tip on one of his cases and had gone back to the police station to follow it up. He knew Rhonda would call him if anything more happened.

Paul was with Barbara right up to the end; he had remained strong for her. In Rhonda's three and a half years at the hospital, she had learned to read people pretty well. She could see that Paul was in no condition to be on his own—he was running on fumes. When she called Mike, she asked him to come by and help their friend get home.

Paul and Barb were also friends with George Carson who was now running his family's funeral home, so the "where" for the funeral was a foregone conclusion. "Stop by and talk to George about the arrangements. I am sure tomorrow will be fine," they told him. He may have heard them—maybe not. He *had* heard when Rhonda told him she had called Mike. She questioned him to make sure he heard her; he assured her that he had. However, he felt a need to be alone just then. After sitting a few minutes, he stood up and walked out. In all the commotion, no one noticed, so when Mike arrived no one knew where Paul was.

Mike drove to the house. Paul did not answer the bell. Mike noticed that the curtains were drawn back and glanced in through the picture window, but he didn't see Paul. Paul's car was not on the street either, but then Mike thought he remembered seeing it as he pulled into the hospital parking lot. He went back. The car was still there but no sign of his friend. He sat in his car for a few minutes and then began to drive around.

With Paul on a different bench from his usual one, Mike missed him at the park. He had seen Paul and Barb on the same bench dozens of times when he made his rounds prior to earning his detective's badge. However, this time Paul sat on another bench over beyond the pine tree that the town always decorated at Christmas. Mike did glance around the park, but the tree obscured his view. He drove down by the river, came back up past the park again, and then went by Paul's office. "Where could he have gone?" he asked himself trying to get into the mind of a man who had just lost his best friend, his wife.

Mike drove around for what seemed like forever. Finally, he ended up back at the house. By that time, Paul had come home, so as Mike walked up the steps and looked through the window, he saw Paul asleep on the couch. "Sleep is what he needs most right now," Mike said to himself. He decided not to ring the bell.

Police Chief Randle had been very excited several weeks before when they installed the car phone the city had approved at last month's meeting. He told the mayor how convenient it would be to get them for the two detectives' cars, but the budget was just too small for that yet. Mike would have to wait to call Rhonda when he got back to the station.

After sitting in the car for a few minutes, he started the engine and headed back to the station to finish some paperwork on that lead. The tip had been a dead end, but he still had to make a report. Besides he needed to make up the time he had missed while he was out looking for Paul.

As he drove, he thought of his two friends, one grieving and the other gone. *His* emotions finally caught up with him too. He had to pull over twice before he got back to the station.

~~~

The morning fit the mood. A cold rain was driven by a north wind. Paul stood at the picture window with a cup of coffee. He had hardly taken a sip. The droplets running down the glass were certainly more numerous than the ones which ran down his face, but they were not as painful.

He contemplated the tasks for the day: the arrangements to be made with the funeral home, taking his suit to the cleaners .... There were so many other things he knew he had to do, but they were just floating around in the back of his mind with neither order nor focus. That was so unlike him; he was the one who was organized and methodical while Barb had been spontaneous and carefree.

"Gosh, I miss her so," he said aloud. As he looked through the window up into the sky, his tears blurred his vision as much as the rain blurred the windowpane.

The phone rang. He reached down to the end table and picked up the receiver. He cleared his throat and was able to get out a "Hello."

"Hey, Paul, it's Mike. I just wanted to see if there is anything I can do."

"No thanks. I just need to run some errands today—get some stuff out of the way."

"Well, do you need a ride to the hospital? You left your car there yesterday."

"Oh ...." Paul glanced out the window and saw that his car was not out at the curb where he usually parked it. He had not even noticed earlier. "Oh, yeah, well, no—no, it's not that far. I'll just walk over when it stops raining."

"Are you sure? The chief says I can take some vacation time if I need to."

"No. I really appreciate it, Mike, but I'll be okay."

"Okay. You know to call me if you need anything."

"Yeah. Thanks Mike. I appreciate all your help. Rhonda's too. You guys have been real friends these last several months."

"Well, Barb and you were really good friends to us too, Paul." After a moment of silence, Mike announced, "Hey, Rhonda said for you to come over for dinner about six tonight. You know she won't take no for an answer. You'll get me in a lot of trouble if you don't come. You know that. Don't leave me hanging, buddy."

Paul chuckled. Mike knew how to get to him. "Okay, okay, but only to save your scrawny little neck." They laughed.

Things were a little better after they hung up. Paul sat down on the couch and sipped his brew. His heart was still heavy, but the phone call had moved his thoughts out of the pain and into the present where he needed to be for the moment.

~~~

Paul had focused on writing and language studies at Wilson Community College. After graduating, he started a freelance business specializing in consulting along with writing proposals and technical reports. He was beginning to develop a strong reputation because of the four very successful advertising campaigns that he had designed in the last year and a half. Under his careful leadership, the business grew quickly. By the time Barbara's cancer had gotten to the point that his efforts at work began to suffer, he had brought in two partners and hired a receptionist, a graphic artist, and a writer. He was upfront about the arrangement with his established clients, and everyone had accepted it as normal business, taking comfort in knowing that Paul was involved in their project at least in an overseer capacity.

After the funeral, Paul took two weeks away from his work to go out to a friend's fishing cabin. He made the decision to go away on a whim. He thought Barbara would have approved, she being the spontaneous half of their whole. His eyes watered at the thought, but the eyes also creased with a half smile generated by fond memories.

While he relaxed at the cabin, he reasoned that as much as he liked their house, the memories would be more than he wanted to deal with. He decided to sell the house and move. When he came home, he looked in his desk, pulled out the business card of a real estate agent he had met through one of his clients, and dialed the number.

"Good morning. Oscar Nance Real Estate," came the cheery voice from the other end.

"Hi. My name is Paul Corning. May I speak to Alice Benson, please?"

"Sure, one moment please." The line clicked several times, then after a brief silence, he heard another click.

"Hello. This is Alice Benson."

"Hi, Miss Benson, this is Paul Corning. We met at the public speaking seminar last year."

"Oh yes, Paul, I remember. You have the advertising agency don't you? How are you doing?"

"Yes, thank you for remembering. Well, not so well actually. My wife died a couple weeks ago …."

"Oh Paul, I'm so sorry," she sympathized, and then said in a surprised tone, "Oh my, now that you mention it, I read about that in the paper. Barbara wasn't it? I just didn't make the connection that she was your wife."

"Yes Ma'am, Barbara."

"Well, I am truly sorry, Paul. I know that you must miss her terribly."

"Yes Ma'am, but that's actually the reason for my call. I think it would be best to sell the house, and I was wondering if I could get with you today to go over the details."

"I would love to, Paul, but I am just heading out to a meeting that will tie me up for the rest of the day. Could we get together tomorrow?"

"Well, actually I am going to Collinsville early in the morning for a presentation and will be gone for the rest of the week," he said. He really did have to get back into his work, and this trip would get his mind off the pain and onto a couple of projects.

Barbara told him several weeks before she died that when she was gone she wanted him to move on with his life. He had swallowed hard when she said that but had said that he would try. "No, promise me," she pressed. He promised.

"I guess it could wait until I got back …"

Alice could sense his hesitation. "Listen. My son-in-law is driving through on his way to Oregon. He is staying the night, and I told him I would make my homemade spaghetti that he likes so much. There is always plenty, so why don't you come over for supper? We can all get acquainted over dinner and then get your paperwork started."

"That sounds wonderful, but I don't want to intrude."

"Not at all. You'll like Tom, and this will get things started on your house."

Paul agreed. She gave him directions and told him to bring an extra key to his house so that she could let an appraiser in and install a lockbox for showing the house. They chatted for a few more minutes and then said their goodbyes.

Chapter 7 – Visits

"I finished with Mr. Simpson's station wagon," Tom said. "It's almost noon. I am going to wash up and get on the road."

"Okay," Frank replied. "By the way, here's a little bonus." He handed Tom an envelope.

"Wow! Thanks! This will help with the trip."

"Well, you've earned it. Debbie was going over the books last night, and she said we have done pretty well these past few months. Your hard work has really helped us a lot. I especially appreciate you coming in this morning before you head out. That puts me in good shape to keep up with routine business until you get back."

"Great! Thanks again. I really appreciate it," Tom said. They shook hands, and Tom went into the back to clean up.

Tom had a real sense of satisfaction. He was pleased that his efforts had been recognized, but more than that, he was pleased that his life was changing. When he worked for Morgan Manufacturing, he was just there for the money—money for the truck, fishing, and beer although not always in that order. However, now he felt like he was not only providing for himself, he was providing a service to his boss and their customers too. It was a good feeling.

"A bonus! How 'bout that?" He chuckled to himself as he pulled down on the rotating cloth towel dispenser and wiped his hands. It was the first bonus he had ever received from a job.

Frank was doing some paperwork at the desk as Tom walked out. "See you in a week," Tom said.

"Okay. Debbie said to tell Liz "Hi" and that Debbie will write as soon as the baby is born. Liz wants to know if it is a boy or a girl."

"I'll tell her. The ladies really get into that pink and blue stuff, don't they?" Tom chuckled.

"Yeah. You know, Debbie and Liz really connected at the dinner after Glenn's funeral, and they started writing every week. Debbie was so excited when she found out that Liz was expecting again last year. And now in another couple of months, we are going to be a mom and dad too."

"That's really neat," Tom said. "You know, the last time I saw little Tommie she was so tiny. They even used her as the baby in the Christmas play at church. Now she is almost six months old. Man, time goes by so fast."

"Tommie! It must be neat to have somebody name their kid after you."

Tom got a huge grin. He could not wait to see 'Lil Punkin', his nickname for her.

"Have a good time, Uncle Tommy. Drive carefully."

"I will," he said, grinning as he walked out the door

Frank finished his paperwork and then walked out into the service bay to start working on Mr. Morley's panel truck.

~~~

Paul had trouble concentrating on his work but was determined to finalize tomorrow's presentation. The Ludlow Company had invited Paul to come over for two days to go over his ideas for the ad campaign. Along with the initial meeting, Paul would meet with two committees within the company to get their thoughts and answer any questions. Then he would wrap things up in a conclusion meeting on the afternoon of the second day. Paul always liked to present several options at the beginning of planning meetings. He found that the more comfortable a company was with his grasp of their needs and the direction he intended to take them, the more latitude they gave him in developing the plan. That had been one of the reasons for the success of his young company which he had steadily built up to five other people.

Paul also spent some time gathering data for the two presentations he would make on his way back from the Ludlow meetings. These were smaller projects, but each company's ventures are important to them whether large or small. Ignoring that fact was a good way to lose a client.

He wrapped up at about half past four and put his papers and sketches into his briefcase. Then he put the case by the front door and started to get ready to go to dinner.

Paul was still a little apprehensive. His job had accustomed him to meeting new people—that was not the problem. He just felt like an outsider intruding on Miss Benson and her relative. However, she had insisted, and it would get the house listed without waiting another whole week.

~~~

Tom stopped to stretch at a rest area on his way to Mom's place. It seemed strange to him that he had called her 'Miss Benson' while he was married to her daughter. It was not until Marsha divorced him that he came to feel comfortable calling her Mom. Their mutual faith had played a part in their familial bond to be sure, but there was a strange irony in the way things worked out. Miss Benson also had a pleasant personality that reminded him of his adopted mom, but somehow that fact had eluded him until these last several months.

He walked around the small park for a few minutes, completely unaware of a chance meeting at this very same place a year and a half before. Marsha's encounter with an older woman and her dog had almost changed her mind about divorcing him.

Before long, Tom was back on the road heading for an encounter with what he considered the finest spaghetti dinner in the entire United States.

~~~

There it was—213 Ogden Wood Lane. Miss Benson's directions had led Paul right to her house.

It was a stone structure, and though the ambience was that of a cottage, that word normally would not be used to describe a house of this size. Set back from the street on a well-manicured lawn, it was surrounded by shade trees that created a charming setting. The flower garden spanning the front was in full display of its spring colors. The whole panorama was what unfolds in the mind while listening to a fairy tale about an undiscovered princess.

Alice Benson had found the place not long after moving to Wellington. Just after Marsha and Tom were married, she was in an automobile accident. Her real estate company hired another agent to help during her four-month recovery. When Alice returned, she found that the office climate had changed, that there was a more aggressive, almost cutthroat atmosphere. That made her uncomfortable, so when she found out about the opening at Oscar Nance Real Estate, she moved to Wellington. This was the fifth house Alice had listed. She wrote up the contract one evening, but the next morning she called the owners and made an offer herself.

A driveway led back to a detached two-car garage just to the rear of the house. There was a car in the driveway already, but Paul did not know whose it was. He did not want to be blocked in since he would be leaving before Miss Benson or her son-in-law, so he parked at the curb.

Even the walkway up to the house maintained the fairy tale atmosphere as it curved its way gently back to the house. Paul stepped up onto the stone porch and rang the doorbell.

A young man answered the door.

"Hello. I'm Paul Corning. Is this Miss Benson's residence?"

"Yes. I'm Tom Jenkins, her son-in-law." Tom reached out his hand. "Come on in," he invited as they shook hands and Paul stepped inside.

"Hi, Paul, it's so nice to see you again." It was Miss Benson coming in from the kitchen. Instead of reaching out to shake his hand, she hugged him. Her voice almost quivered when she repeated the sympathies she had offered Paul earlier on the phone.

"Thank you," Paul said. "This has been a very hard time for me; I appreciate your kindness in having me over this evening. Also, thanks for helping me with the house." 'Helping with the house' as he put it is what she did for a living, but she understood that he was expressing appreciation for having him over after-hours, although it wasn't as if real estate agents actually worked regular hours.

"Can I help with the table, Mom?"

"No. No, I have it all set. You guys sit down and get acquainted." Tom sat on the couch and motioned Paul to take the easy chair.

"Now that you are both here, I will put on the spaghetti and be right back. The water is already heated, so it won't be long."

From the time they each arrived, the men were enticed by the aroma of the homemade sauce which made the whole house smell like a kitchen in Tuscany. "Just wait until you taste it, Paul. The experience is the only thing better than the anticipation."

Alice grinned at Tom's comment as she walked into the kitchen. She soon had the pasta in the water and the timer set. By the time she was back, the conversation had moved over to Paul's recent loss.

Tom seemed genuinely concerned. "May I ask you a personal question, Paul?"

"Yes."

Without delay Tom asked, "Are you a Christian?"

"Yes," Paul replied. Then before it was asked, he answered Tom's next question. "So was Barbara. The one bright spot in this whole thing is that I know I will see her again someday."

"Yeah," Tom commented with a big grin, sitting back on the sofa and folding his hands behind his head. "There is a lot of comfort in knowing that."

Even with blurry eyes, Paul could not help but smile. This was turning out to be a good evening. And Tom was right—the homemade meatballs and spaghetti was spectacular!

~~~

Paul awoke early in the morning and started out on his journey. There was time to get to the Ludlow offices for his 10:30 meeting but not a lot of time to spare. He had intended to drive over last night, but the new friendships he made with Alice and Tom were a precious salve to his hurting soul. He had not left Alice's until after ten last night.

Arriving at Ludlow's with twenty-three minutes to spare, Paul made his presentation and was very pleased with the response. Charles Ludlow was very complimentary. The younger Ludlow brother Randolph mentioned that Paul was quickly convincing him they made the right move in dropping the big advertising firm they had been with for the last twelve years. The older of the two men had learned the business under the tutelage of their father and now ran the aging founder's company. The younger of the two studied at Parker's Lake Business School and ran the financial side of things.

Paul was energized by the good reactions he received. He spent the evening in his hotel room weaving the new ideas from the day into his closing presentation. He also anticipated some of the questions he would garner tomorrow and the data he would receive. Additionally, he would try to anticipate the unexpected in his closing comments.

This was going to be the most ambitious project his young firm had ever undertaken. He had used several other freelancers on various projects during Barbara's illness, and he would have to bring them in full time for at least a month in order to stay on schedule. When he was satisfied with his summation, he reviewed the presentations he would make on his way back home for his clients in Quincy on Thursday and Parker's Lake on Friday.

~~~

As on his two previous trips, Tom's visit with the Websters was a delight. He took Melissa and Little Glenn out to the pond for some fishing. During his visit last summer, Melissa had been squeamish about baiting her hook, but this time, it just seemed to be second nature to her. On the other hand, even though doing bodily harm to a worm was second nature to rough-and-tumble Little Glenn, he was still a little young to be dealing with the business end of a hook. Tom did the honors.

Ben and Liz were such an inspiration and encouragement to Tom: in his faith, but also to his life in general. It was not as obvious to him, but he encouraged them too. The Websters had been tested by three deaths over recent years, and even though two of them occurred before they were Christians, they were able to pass some of the lessons they learned on to their new friend in his struggle with their mutual loss of Glenn. Additionally, though they would never personally need the skills to deal with the disintegration of their own family, they would learn through Tom's experience ways to encourage and help others who were struggling with divorce—that deep, inner war from which none escape unharmed.

Tom would be leaving on Saturday. As a treat, Friday after lunch, Tom took the kids to town to get some ice cream. Melissa reminded him of Uncle Glenn's spilled milkshake incident and warned him, through a big grin of course, that they would tell Mom and Dad if he repeated Uncle Glenn's blunder. They all laughed hardily. Melissa was learning well the lessons her parents were modeling before her: that of teasing without hurting; of laughing with, but not at; of brightening the world, not casting shadows upon it. It reminded Tom of the plaque hanging in their hallway which read simply, "Live. Laugh. Love."

Tom silently lifted his heart in praise to God for allowing him to be a part of this dear family. God had allowed Tom to be a part of his family too; Tom also thanked him for that.

~~~

"Bye, kids. I sure am gonna miss you guys."

Breakfast was over. The car was packed. The only things left were the hugs and kisses and the promises to return.

"Now, ya be careful drivin' on the way home, Tommy," Liz instructed. "The kids need ya, an' me an' Ben too."

"Okay, 'Mother'," he assured her, exaggerating his words with a grin. "I'll be careful." She gave him a jab in the ribs, and he howled with laughter, then suddenly shushed himself so as not to awaken little Tommie, asleep in Liz's arms.

After a tearful hug from Liz, she admonished, "Do be careful."

"I will." Then came a hearty handshake from Ben, more hugs from the kids, and a gentle kiss on Lil Punkin's precious forehead, softly, so as not to wake her.

Tom got in the car and started down the dirt drive that connected the house to the rural road that bordered their twenty-seven-acre family haven. With a wave out the window as he pulled onto the road, he was homeward bound.

~~~

Tom pulled into Alice's driveway a little after seven o'clock. He got out of the car and started across the walkway in front of the house. As he stepped up onto the porch, he saw that the front door was open. He knocked on the wooden frame of the screen door and called out, "Mom?"

"Come in, Tom."

He pulled back the screen door and stepped in to see his mother-in-law wiping her eyes with a handkerchief. "Are you okay?" he asked. "What happened?"

She sat reflectively for a moment and then said, "I have something to tell you, Tom. Please, sit down." Not sure what to expect, he took a seat in the easy chair.

After a pause, Alice brushed the hair out of her face and looked at him. "I …" She choked on the word, cleared her throat, and began again. "I know you were hoping that after a separation maybe Marsha would come around and want to put things back together with you." She looked down. "I was praying for that too." She paused, and then she looked back up at him, the tears flowing again. "Tom—she got married last night."

He sat there, not sure what to say. A Vietnam monsoon was flooding his mind… "I don't understand. She's in South Carolina. How did you get back so fast?"

She hung her head and began to shake with quiet sobs. The pitch of her voice rose as she attempted to speak through her tears. "She didn't invite me, Tom. She said she knew I wouldn't approve of him, so she didn't invite me."

"Why didn't you at least tell me what was going on when I was here?" He was not accusing her; he just didn't understand.

"I didn't know it, Tom. She called me this afternoon. That was the first that I knew of it. She never even told me she was seeing anybody."

Tom was dumbfounded and sat without speaking. Slowly, it dawned on him that Alice was as hurt at being cut out of her daughter's life as he was by the news of Marsha's marriage. He got up out of the chair and sat down on the couch beside her, putting his arm around her shoulders.

"I know there isn't much I can say that will help right now, but just remember that God is doing something. Somehow—somehow he's doing something. Cry if you need to, but don't despair. Somehow God is doing something."

She reached over to her shoulders and put her hand on top of his, but she continued to weep, dabbing her eyes with her handkerchief.

When the mood softened a bit, he said, "Hey, why don't we go out for dinner? My boss gave me a bonus before I left. Did I tell you that?"

"No," she said with a weak laugh, wiping her eyes again.

"Well, he did. I thought I was going to need it on the trip, but I had enough money without it. Let's go blow it all on a night on the town. We can go to that steak place on High Street. Then we can get some ice cream and really make a night of it. And then …." The more he talked, the more animated he got. The more animated he got, the more she giggled. The more she giggled, the more he played up the whole thing until they were both laughing hysterically.

"Come on, let's go," he urged.

"Okay. I hadn't started dinner when she called, and I didn't feel like it afterward. But only if I buy, okay?"

"You can pay for the ice cream, but tonight I am taking my mom out to dinner!"

She blushed at his tender kindness in her time of sorrow, especially knowing that Tom was dealing with sorrow of his own. "One day Marsha will regret losing this man," she thought as she walked toward the bathroom to repair her face from several hours of crying. As she got to the hall, she stopped and turned. "You're a good man, Tom," she said, sorrow still showing on her face.

"And you're a good mom," he responded.

~~~

"Wow, this is a nice place," Tom said as they walked into The Laredo Bunkhouse, the steak place he had only seen from the road. It had been built with a rustic look so that from the outside, it had the appearance of age. However, inside it was very comfortable. They took their seat in a booth. After a brief time, a waitress came over. "What can I get you to drink?" she asked and began to list several beers.

"I'll have an RC Cola," Tom said. "What do you want, Mom?"

"I'll just have water."

"Come on. We are out on the town tonight. Get something besides water."

Alice laughed, "No, I really want water."

"Okay, one water and a RC," Tom said. The waitress brought the drinks back and took their food orders.

As they talked, Alice mentioned that she had sold this property to the developers who built the restaurant.

"Really?" Tom marveled.

"Yes, this was my first commercial deal. I had only sold residential deals in Johnstown, but this opportunity fell into my lap just after I moved here. Before I knew it, the deal was done. I mean literally—about two weeks from contract to closing. I even used part of my commission on this place as a down payment on my house. They started construction a couple months later and opened that September."

"How neat is that!" Tom exclaimed. "So, you know these people?"

"No. The people I dealt with worked out of Amarillo. They are setting up a series of restaurants all over the Southwest. This is as far north as they have come so far, but they plan to branch out all across the country."

"I'll bet you would like to get in on all *those* deals."

"You *know* it!" she chuckled.

Their meals arrived, and they continued talking and laughing. Alice was surprised to find out about Tom's near-fatal accident. It happened during the beginning of the end, and Marsha never mentioned it to her mom, perhaps because she didn't want to arouse any sympathy for him. Tom had not become close to Alice until several months later, and the subject simply had never come up.

Tom wondered if Marsha had ever told her about Linh. Alice told him that Marsha never mentioned a name, but she did accuse him of committing adultery while he was in Vietnam. It hurt him to hear it put that way, but deep down he knew that no matter what words were used, that *was* what he did. Adultery. Plain and simple. It was one of the many sins for which he had needed to ask forgiveness.

He stopped eating and sat staring at the table. Alice saw a cloud of melancholy settling over him. He looked up at her after she called his name the second time. "You're thinking about it right now, aren't you?"

He looked back at the table. "I messed up so bad, Mom."

She paused, searching for the right words. "Look, Tom. There is no excuse for what you did. I wish you hadn't done it, but I am sure *you* wish you hadn't done it too. Right?" He nodded, head still down.

She continued, "Tom, God has a way of taking the things we mess up and making something good come from it. He says that 'All things work together for good to them that love God, to them who are the called according to his purpose'." (Romans 8:28)

"Like what? What good could possibly come from such a terrible thing?"

"Well, Tom, would you be a Christian today if Marsha hadn't left you?"

Silence.

"No, I guess not," he finally answered softly, the truth beginning to dawn on him.

"Actually, God has his ways, Tom. Even if Marsha and you were still married, God could have taken you down some other path to bring you to himself. But God took your life as it was and used the events in it as part of his plan to work his will in your life."

"But I messed it up so bad."

"Yes. The pain and destruction which we bring on ourselves and inflict on others when we go our own way demonstrates why we should follow God's ways and not our own. We should never use God's mercy as an excuse to sin, nor does his forgiveness guarantee that our actions will not cause real and long-lasting consequences." Tom was still looking down at the table when Alice sighed, "But God will use our mistakes, and even our sins, to bring good to those who will trust in Him."

"But sometimes, it's so hard to forgive myself."

"I know, Tom, and like I said before, we should take sin very seriously because God takes it seriously. It took the death of his Son on the cross to solve that problem. What we must remember is that God not only knows the depth of our sin, he also knows the value of his redemption. If God says you are forgiven, Tom," she nodded her head and raised her eyebrows, "then you are forgiven."

A peace warmed his heart much like the one he knew when he first trusted in Christ. In the days since then, he had sensed that same peace anytime his heart focused on the Lord; however, that peace faded to apprehension, fear, and anger anytime his thoughts centered on himself, his troubles, his circumstances, or other lesser things.

As hard as it was to forgive himself, he knew that Alice was right. "Help me trust you, Father," he whispered in his heart.

The mood lightened as they talked some more and finished their meal. Suddenly, Tom got a gleam in his eye and announced that it was time for ice cream. Alice laughed hard when Tom relayed the third-hand tale of Glenn's milkshake debacle. "That must have embarrassed him no end to have his own instructions come back to haunt him like that," Alice sympathized, "especially since he had to wear the evidence right out front where everyone could see it."

"Yeah. If Nathaniel Hawthorne were alive today, he could write a sequel, *The Chocolate Letter*!" More laughter and giggling bubbled up between them until they feared they were drawing the attention of everyone around them. They paid their bill, laughed their way to the car, and headed toward the ice cream parlor.

Chapter 8 – The Idea

Tom could not remember a more gorgeous Sunday morning in a long time. He thought of Pastor Wayne and prayed for his friends back in Johnstown. He would return there later today, but this morning he would go to church with Alice as he had done the other times he stayed with her on his way back from Oregon.

They were good people at Alice's church in Wellington. They had welcomed him enthusiastically as her guest on each occasion. It spoke well of the congregation that they welcomed strangers. It also spoke of their respect for Miss Benson. She had been going there since she moved to town and had brought with her a letter of high commendation from the church in Johnstown where she had been a member since she became a Christian at the age of twelve.

They drove separately since Tom would head home from there.

This morning there was a guest speaker, Robert DeKirk, who was a semi-retired missionary with a vision for a different kind of mission support. He envisioned a network of people all across the country who would be involved in aggressive behind-the-scenes efforts.

"We need people out 'in the field' as we often call it," Mr. DeKirk said. "And here in our own country, we need the Lord's people involved in praying and giving. All too often, we think that it stops there, but it doesn't my dear brothers and sisters." He gave an illustration of a military operation: "There are many soldiers in field positions, but they require a number of people *behind* the lines, and even back in the home country, who are vital to sustain the efforts of the front line troops. They provide a constant flow of food, equipment, and supplies." Tom understood from personal experience what he was saying and remembered running low on ammo during the ambush. It was a cause of increasing gratitude that he no longer became angry when he recalled those days.

The speaker continued speaking, saying familiar *and* new things to Tom. "That supply-line mindset is what I hope I can help you to see this morning because it is the same way in missions. We need folks at home who can pray, who can give, and who can write letters of encouragement. But oh, my friends, I would have you grasp a vision for the abundance of other opportunities. Could you fold, address, and send out newsletters? Could you set up a prayer chain so when one person hears of a prayer request, it quickly reaches a large number of prayer warriors?"

He was a particularly good speaker, not creating guilt but rather stirring interest and excitement, vision and passion, in both field and support opportunities.

He spoke for a few more minutes on other, often overlooked opportunities. Then, he closed the message about ten minutes before the normal time—an act that prompted some to tease their pastor that this fellow should be invited to speak more often.

By the end of the service, Tom's head was reeling with things he had never thought of before, but particularly with one idea that he was eager to discuss with Mr. DeKirk. The church was having a potluck meal after the service. Tom held back until the crowd around the speaker had dispersed and then asked if he could join him at the dinner table. It reminded Tom of a similar dinner almost a year and a half ago when he asked to sit with Wayne Hamilton. Little did he know that this meal would change his life as much as the meal with Wayne had.

~~~

Tom walked Alice to her car, mentioning the thoughts he had discussed with Mr. DeKirk. "That sounds wonderful, Tom. What was his reaction?"

"He thought it was a good idea and told me I should get started on it."

"Well, how are you going to start?"

"But Mom, I didn't tell him about it to get his blessings on *my* efforts. I just thought if it was a good idea, he might know someone who could do it. I can't do something like that. It would take planning and coordination and … and …. I wouldn't know where in the world to start or how to organize it. Or *anything*!"

"You told me your boss at the service station is a Christian. Would he be interested?"

Tom thought for a minute. "I didn't think of that. I guess I'll have to ask him, but I still wouldn't know how to get started. I just gave Mr. DeKirk the idea for somebody else."

"Sometimes," Alice commented, "God gives one person an idea he intends for another. But many times, God gives an idea to the one he intends to carry it out." There was a pause. Then she said, "Pray about it Tom. 'If any of you lack wisdom, let him ask of God, that giveth to all men liberally, and upbraideth not; and it shall be given him'." (James 1:5)

They stood there for a moment. Then Tom said a hesitant, "Okay, but you pray too. I don't know what I am doing with this."

"I will pray, Tom. Let me know when God starts working things out. Also, let me know if I can do something to help, even though I would be more lost about it than you are."

He opened her car door, and she swung her purse over to the passenger seat, but instead of getting into the car, she turned around and put her hands on his shoulders. "You're a good man, Tom. I think of you more as a son than a son-in-law." She thought again of Marsha and whispered a prayer.

"Thanks Mom," he smiled. "I feel the same way."

Alice got into her car, and Tom closed her door. They exchanged waves, and she pulled out toward the road as he got into his car.

"*Me* in *missions*! That's *crazy*," he chuckled. He started the engine and headed out on the last four hours of a very pleasant and very memorable trip.

~~~

It was another glorious morning in Johnstown. Tom had never been a morning person, but he was progressively finding it easier to awake excited about the new day. He sat on the edge of the bed grinning at how good everything seemed. He mused, "I must have tricked somebody somewhere out of their good day because this is more good-day than one person should be having."

He really enjoyed his trips to Oregon, but he was particularly anxious to get back to work this time. He wanted to talk to Frank about his idea and see what he thought.

Tom almost floated as he showered and got dressed, then headed out the door for breakfast with Wayne.

~~~

As Tom pulled into the station, he was amused that in his excitement, he had actually beaten Frank to work today. He unlocked the door, hung up his jacket, turned on the lights, and started looking at the planning board Frank had set up to keep track of each car. Next to the hook for the car keys, the board listed what was awaiting parts, when the parts were due in, the customer's name and phone number.

He picked the next project, took the keys from the planning board, walked out into the bay, and opened the overhead door. As he walked into the parking area to pull the car in, Frank rounded the corner and pull into the station. They smiled and waved to each other. Then Tom waited for his boss to get out of the car.

"Now see here, Mr. Richards," Tom said in an authoritative voice, "it appears that you are falling behind in your duties. I think you're going to have to stop letting your valuable employees take so much time off!"

Frank grinned and slapped Tom on the arm. "I did miss your help while you were gone. How was the trip?"

"Really good," he said. "There's an idea I want to talk to you about at lunch."

"All right. The sign at the diner said they were having the meatloaf special for lunch today. I'll run up at noon and pick up a couple of orders; then we can sit and talk."

"Great."

"How are the Websters?"

"They were just as happy as ever. And Lil Punkin is so cute, Frank, and so big. I couldn't believe how much she's grown; she'll be walking before I see her again."

"Yeah, kids are like that. I really look forward to having our own little critter running around the house."

"Little Critter! I see you've already picked out a nickname."

Frank laughed. "Okay, Uncle Tommy, let's get to work."

"Yes sir, Boss," he said with a grin and a snappy salute. He got into the car, started it up, and pulled it into the bay.

~~~

Tom had just finished a tire rotation and balancing when Frank walked through the door with the two lunch specials.

"It looks like Mr. Hannan's car probably needs some new front-end parts and an alignment too," Tom announced. "Things are getting a little loose under there."

"Okay, I'll call him after lunch and see if he wants to do that now or schedule it later."

Tom stepped outside to get two Nehi orange sodas from the vending machine. Frank was already enjoying his first mouthful when Tom returned with the soft drinks.

"Okay, what did you want to talk about?" Frank asked.

Tom placed one orange drink on Frank's desk, picked up the paper sack containing his food, and sat down in a chair in the corner.

"Well, they had a missionary speaker at Miss Bennett's church yesterday, and he had some really neat ideas, Frank." Tom went on to outline Mr. DeKirk's message and mentioned that he had discussed an idea with the speaker. He told Frank the silly notion that Mr. DeKirk and Miss Bennett thought that Tom was the one to carry it out.

"Okay, what's the idea?" Frank inquired.

"Well, what if there was a way that when missionaries came home on furlough that they could get tune ups and oil changes for just for the cost of material? What if we could get a bunch of Christian owned service stations all across the country to agree to do that? Maybe other Christians could raise donations so that the missionaries wouldn't even have to pay for parts. Perhaps, there would even be enough money so that service stations could maintain a pool of cars for missionaries to borrow while they were on furlough so they wouldn't even have to think about a car at all when they came back."

Frank grinned at Tom's extensive explanation and evident enthusiasm.

"What's so funny?" Tom demanded with a smile of his own.

"I think the missionary and your mother-in-law are right. I think you *are* the man for the job."

"Not me, I meant *you* could start something like that. You already own a station, and you know people in the business. You could do this, Frank."

"Well, I could help. I would be willing to sign on with you, Tom, but you're the one with all the excitement, all the passion."

"I don't know how to do that kind of thing, Frank. I am not trained in missionary kind of stuff. I'm just a mechanic!"

"Tom, nobody is trained in anything until they get trained."

Tom laughed at how obvious the thought was. "I guess not. It's just that I wouldn't even know where to start."

Frank took another bite of mashed potatoes. "Well, when you are doing something that no one has ever done before, then *nobody* knows where to start. You just feel your way along in the dark until you begin to see some light. We *do* have an advantage, Tom. We can ask God where to start and if this is something God wants you do."

"Yeah, that's what Miss Benson said except she poked me with that verse about asking the Lord for wisdom and Him not holding back. Then Wayne said the same thing this morning at breakfast and also added the one in Proverbs about trusting in the Lord with all your heart and not leaning on your own understanding." Then Tom let out with a big laugh. "I guess if I am going to ask you guys a question, I better be ready for the answer."

Frank laughed too. "I guess you'd better."

Before they went back to work, they prayed and asked God for wisdom and direction in whatever he wanted them to do.

Chapter 9 – Meeting of Minds

During the ensuing weeks, Tom did a lot of fishing. He thought more clearly when he was fishing. He smiled at how much *more* clearly he thought when he was not drinking while he was fishing! But even though ideas were rolling around in his head, he never could see how the pieces all fit together.

The summertime activities kept things moving fast enough that he was not giving his idea much thought. Then one Sunday in late July, Pastor Wayne suggested they go over to the lake on Friday for a little fishing trip. The church was having a missionary speaker the next Sunday, so Wayne did not have to prepare a sermon. The thought of a day on the lake with a rod and reel was enticing to both of them. "I'll check with Frank about taking the day off," Tom said.

~~~

"Hi, Paul; this is Bill Blakley of Fenton & Brown."

"Oh hi, Bill. How are you?"

"Doing well, Paul. And you?"

"Quite well, thank you. I just finished a major project and am enjoying a little calm before the next storm."

"Well," Bill chuckled. "I may be your next storm." He was one of the top dogs at the company in Parker's Lake where Paul had made his presentation almost two months ago. Paul had brought up some new ideas that the company had never considered; however, they had decided that they needed to pull back and reevaluate the direction they wanted to take their company.

"We've thought about your ideas, and we're ready to pull the trigger, Paul. We're wondering when you can come back to go over the details."

"Great. I'll be driving over to visit my folks tomorrow and could stop by Friday afternoon on my way back if that works for you."

"Fair enough. Shall we say two o'clock then? That will give us time to review things, and then we can deal with questions over supper."

They ended the call with cordialities.

Paul did not mention it to his client, but even though completing the Ludlow project had been his biggest business success ever, it was surprisingly unfulfilling. There was just something missing. He still missed his dear wife with whom he once enjoyed sharing his victories. Mike Baker gladly became an open ear for his friend. On more than one occasion, Paul had confided, "It's just not the same without her."

~~~

"Ready to go?" Wayne was right on time.

"I am always ready to go fishing!" Tom replied with a smile, grabbing his cap and sunglasses as he headed out the door. As they walked to Wayne's car, Tom stopped to get the fishing gear from his trunk. Soon they were on the road.

"Did you call your mother-in-law?" Wayne asked, following up on an earlier conversation. Parker's Lake was only about an hour from Wellington where Alice Benson lived. Tom had asked if he could invite her to meet them in town for lunch before they headed to the lake for the afternoon. Wayne thought it was a great idea. Tom always spoke highly of Miss Benson, and it would be nice to meet her.

"Yes. She's going to meet us at Darla's Diner at noon. I've never eaten there, but I have driven past it on my way to Wellington. I'll show you where it is when we get into town."

They drove on for a few moments, and then Wayne added, "I don't think I ever mentioned to you that I have lunch with the pastor of Spring Hill Church every month or so. I mentioned you to him when you started coming to our church, and he said that he remembered you, that he performed your wedding ceremony. He said that Miss Benson was a member there until she moved out of town."

"Yeah," Tom replied. "I forgot about them with all the struggles I had with Marsha, but they were always friendly to me."

As they drove, they passed Pete's Place. Tom's head turned as they passed. Then he grew quiet.

"What's the matter?" Wayne asked.

"I used to go to that bar back there."

"The one back on the left?"

"Yeah. I can't imagine how much time and money I must have spent there." Tom gave a sheepish laugh and shook his head.

"Do you miss it?"

"No, actually I don't. Sometimes I just wonder about my old buddies." Tom had learned that he could speak freely with Wayne. "It is kinda strange though that there are some things that I used to do that the Lord changed in me very quickly—almost immediately. Other things I still struggle with."

Before Glenn's death, Tom's idea of Christianity was that it was just judgmental, self-righteous, and "Do this and don't do that." After he experienced God's mercy in his own life, he found that other Christians were pretty much just plain folks like him. They genuinely loved God, but they had their share of struggles and problems. Just like unbelievers, Christians grapple with unrealized dreams, self-doubts, and regrets. They have mortgages; they work and take care of their families. The difference was that Christians knew that God was doing something in their lives that gave them purpose. It was not completely clear to Tom exactly *what* God was doing; it was like pieces of a puzzle that don't always seem to fit together, but he *had* seen enough of God's hand in his life that his faith was strong in good times and even grew as he went through difficulties.

Tom's comment about struggling with other things elicited a little grunt from Wayne. "God does do things in a strange way sometimes. I have been a Christian for more than 25 years, Tom, and I can tell you that God's ways surely are above our ways," he said, restating a passage in the book of Isaiah.

"Yeah, and God's ways are past finding out," Tom replied, quoting another passage, this one in Romans.

Their minds wandered off into the wonder of their God and his marvelous ways, not the least of which is God's tender mercies to undeserving people who simply trust in Him.

An hour before they got to Parker's Lake, they passed several fields of wheat. As far back as he could remember, it had been a marvel to Tom that a farmer could put a tiny piece of grain into the ground and over time it multiplied many times. Since the time of his faith, however, wheat fields also reminded him of the passage in the Bible where Jesus used the kernel of wheat falling into the ground and dying as a picture of himself laying down his own life so that many people would come to forgiveness and faith in God. That illustration would become more real to Tom as the days and months unfolded before him.

~~~

"There it is." Tom pointed across the road to their left. Wayne found a parking spot and pulled in. They got out of the car and began to cross the street.

Watching out through the restaurant window, Alice said, "Tom will be so surprised to see you here."

As they entered the diner, Tom looked around the room for a friendly face, but his eyes met two of them instead.

"Hi, Mom," he said walking over and giving her a hug. "And Brother Paul," he continued, reaching out his hand. "What brings you to the fine town of Parker's Lake?"

"Business, actually," Paul replied. "I have a meeting with a client this afternoon. I came in here to get a bite before the presentation, and who do you think I met here?" He motioned to Alice who sat there grinning.

Tom said how glad he was to see them both and then introduced Wayne.

Lunch was a pleasant time of refreshing, of new and renewed friendships. The restaurant was clean and had the appearance of being newly remodeled. The meal was delicious. The home-cooked style food was served by a pleasant, middle-aged lady with what was obviously prematurely graying hair.

As they ate, Alice asked, "Well, Tom, how is your mission project coming along? I am still praying for you. How is the Lord working that out?"

"Well, Mom, I can't seem to get anything going. I keep thinking about it, but I don't know where to start."

"But Tom, you work with cars everyday," Alice said.

"Working on the cars is one thing, Mom. Building an organization to service cars for free all across the country is something quite different."

"Or around the world," Wayne added.

"Huh?"

"Around the world, Tom. Missionaries need transportation all around the world, not just here in the States."

"Do you see what I mean? That is just too much for me to do!"

Paul spoke up, "Miss Benson was telling me about your idea, Tom, and I think it is a good one. You should do it."

"Yeah, but I just can't do it. Everyone thinks I am the one who is supposed to do it, just because I had the idea."

"Well," Paul continued, "maybe you *are* supposed to do it, but maybe you aren't supposed to do it by yourself."

"Wha … what do you mean?" Though Tom was among friends who were truly interested, he remained a little defensive.

Paul appeared reflective for a moment. "Maybe other people are supposed to help you."

Wayne watched the conversation unfold for a few minutes then sat forward in his chair. "I had not thought of this angle before, but this conversation reminds me of chapter 12 in First Corinthians where God uses the human body as an illustration of how his work is to be done here in the world. Do you recall that if we were all 'eyes', we would not be able to hear? And if we were all 'ears', we would not be able to smell? Different people have different gifts and should all work together to accomplish God's purposes."

"Yeah, you taught about that last year, a few months after I started coming to church," Tom replied.

"Okay. Now you work at Frank's station don't you, Tom?"

"Yeah."

"So you actually work on the cars."

"Yeah. And some trucks too," he added.

"And you do all the paperwork?"

"Well, I write down what I did. We call it a 'history card'. Frank works on the cars too, but he also uses the history cards to write out the bills."

"So you and Frank do the mechanical work, and then Frank also does the billing and the accounting?"

"Actually, Frank makes out the bills, but Debbie does the accounting."

"Okay. Are you starting to see where I am going with this?" Wayne asked. "Look at how the responsibilities are divided up. You would probably be lost if you had to do the accounting, but Debbie never comes to church with grease under her fingernails, does she?" He let his rhetorical question sink in. "In other words, Debbie does not do tune ups or rebuild engines, does she?"

"No." Tom chuckled, starting to let his guard down.

"Of course not. The place would not function very well if she didn't do what she does, but she wouldn't have anything to do at all if you and Frank didn't do what you do."

"That is a neat illustration," Paul said. "It makes more sense now in light of the Corinthians passage. I mean, I never thought of it before, but I do it all the time. If I am short on time or need some specialized research prepared, I delegate work to someone or hire other people with expertise that my company doesn't have."

"Yeah," Alice added. "We do that also. Last month, we had Paul come to our real estate agency to give us ideas on better marketing."

"Exactly," Wayne said. "Tom, maybe we should not be praying that God would show you if you are supposed to do this impossible task. Perhaps what we should be praying for is that if God wants you to do the project that he would bring you into contact with the people that could help you do the impossible."

There was a brief silence, then Paul let out a quiet, "Ouch."

"What's the matter, Paul?" Alice asked.

"I just got the sneaking idea that I may be one of the people God might want to use on this project."

Wayne and Alice laughed. "Do you see that, Tom?" Wayne questioned. "God is answering our prayer, and we haven't even asked yet!" More smiles and chuckling emerged.

As they continued to talk, their four hearts began melding in both an attitude of thanksgiving for mercies provided and an attitude of dedication to serve the God from whom those mercies had come.

Paul jotted down Tom's phone number and promised to call him Sunday afternoon to discuss the idea in more detail. By the time they parted, Tom was feeling that if God was in it, maybe the impossible was possible after all!

~~~

The trip back to Johnstown was even more exciting than the trip to Parker's Lake. Pleasant memories of the relaxing fishing trip became enhanced by the anticipation that God was actually going to utilize Tom somehow.

Christians often go through several phases in their journey of faith. First is the realization that nobody is so good that they don't need God's forgiveness nor so bad that God will not forgive those who trust him. As time goes by, believers start wanting to do something for the Lord in order to show gratitude for that mercy and grace. Then somewhere along the journey, Christians finally come to realize that God is not calling them to do something *for* him. Instead, God wants them to yield as a tool in his hand and trust him to do something *through* them. God calls it being "instruments of righteousness" (Romans 6:13), like a scalpel is an instrument of good when used by a skilled surgeon.

Tom began to sense that he was on a journey of discovering that his weakness was going to give rise to God's strength; that his inability was going to be the stage on which God would display His ability. The excitement energized Tom, even more than the dread once discouraged him.

~~~

Tom found a parking place at the restaurant and got out of the car. He approached the door at the same time as an elderly couple and opened it for them. "Thank you, young man," the woman said; the man nodded his head toward Tom. As they entered, a young lady with a little boy at her side and a younger girl in her arms was leaving. Tom continued to hold the door for the trio, and the woman likewise expressed appreciation.

As Tom entered, he thought about the last time he was at The Ranch on that Thanksgiving Day with Marsha. It was not quite two years ago, but it seemed like so much longer. He thought about it for a moment and remembered that on that very same evening Frank had called out his name, changing his life forever.

As he scanned the room looking for Paul, a waving hand caught his eye. It was Brenda Baker, his former classmate and his former nurse.

"Hi, Brenda," he said walking up to her table. They had met in passing several times since Tom became a Christian, and the tense memories quickly dissolved into non-memories as they rejoiced together in their common faith. At first, it annoyed him to admit that she had been right, but he quickly realized how silly the thought was. He now knew beyond a shadow of doubt that he *did* need God! The thought soon became a source for many a thankful grin cast heavenward.

"Hi yourself, stranger. Long time, no see. How've you been?"

"I'm actually doing very well thanks. God is doing some neat stuff right now. How about you?"

"I'm well also. Do you have time to tell me about it?"

"Actually, I am meeting a friend for lunch to go over some ideas, but he's not here yet." Tom sat down and began to tell her about the thoughts he had and some of the preliminary concepts he had discussed with Paul about the car service ministry.

Brenda listened attentively as he made his informal presentation. Then she sat back with a big grin and said, "So Doubting Thomas is becoming a missionary. How about that?" They both laughed.

They talked for a few minutes until Paul arrived. Tom made the introductions, and then excused Paul and himself from Brenda's table.

"Why don't you just eat here?" she asked, adding with a grin, "I'm interested in missions too, ya know."

The waiter noticed the growing group at the table and came by to take the additional orders. After a good meal complemented with good conversation, Paul took a composition book from his case and started to share his thoughts.

~~~

It had been another beautiful Sunday. Tom spent the morning with Wayne and the friends he considered his church family, but tonight he and Paul were visiting another church.

He arrived thirty minutes early to meet with Paul and help set up a literature table. As the singing started, Tom's nerves kicked into overdrive. Just then Paul leaned over and reminded him of their discussions about relaxing and remembering that these people were his family, fellow Christians who were interested in what Paul and he had to say. They spoke quietly for a few minutes. Paul went over the points Tom was to cover and assured him everything was going to be all right.

The last strains of "Because He Lives" flowed through the sanctuary. The music director smiled and welcomed those who were visiting for the first time. He then gave a rising motion with his hands and said, "All right, let's all stand and say our memory verse for this month. Ready? 'This is the day which the LORD hath made; we will rejoice and be glad in it. Psalm 118:24.' Very good, you may be seated." He gave the page number for another hymn. There was a brief moment of rustling pages, and then the organ began to play the introductory notes of "Amazing Grace".

Tom thought of the previous times he had been in that auditorium: when he was dating Marsha, for their wedding, and for the Christmas play. Except for the wedding, they always sat toward the back. He would spend the time wondering when things would be over. Now here he was, deliberately sitting on the front row and about to be introduced as one of the speakers for the evening. He chuckled to himself with an ironic smile and shook his head in wonder at the amazing grace God had displayed in reaching down and not only saving him from certain ruin, but also in moving in Tom's life to bring glory to Himself.

Suddenly in the middle of that glorious thought, Tom realized the cause for his great anxiety. It was not just the speaking or the new surroundings, though both did concern him. It was his past. He was worried about how people would react to him, to the divorce, to his drinking, to all the things he thought they might hold against him.

"Lord, I can't do this. I just can't do this," he protested silently.

Then that verse came back to him once again and settled in his heart: "My strength is made perfect in weakness."

After the announcements and another song, Pastor Copley stood and walked to the front of the platform. "I want to introduce to you a young man some of you may remember. He has visited with us before, but this time he has come back to speak to us about a unique missions opportunity. Please welcome Tom Jenkins."

The applause was encouraging to his frightened soul. He stood up on trembling legs and made his way up the steps to the platform. As he stopped at the lectern and turned toward the congregation, to his surprise, he saw his mother-in-law seated in the third row applauding him on to his task. They had announced Tom and Paul's planned visit several weeks ago, and one of Alice's friends had called to let her know. She had driven all the way from Wellington just to be there. Seated next to her was one of the young ladies who had been in Miss Benson's fifth grade Sunday School class fourteen years earlier— Brenda Baker. Brenda was applauding too, and they both were beaming.

Just as he had planned it with Paul, Tom's presentation was brief. In another four minutes, he had given a short outline of his plan and introduced Paul who filled in the details before inviting Pastor Copley and his congregation to join them in this new missions support venture. The positive response surprised Tom, and he mentioned it to Pastor Copley after the meeting.

"Well, one of our missionaries retired from his work in Cameroon," the pastor said. "Recently he has been going around the country encouraging churches to get involved in missions support projects. We had him here early last month, and it created a lot of interest. When Wayne Hamilton told me about the work you and Paul were starting, it seemed like the Lord's leading to have you fellows over to tell us what you were doing."

Tom anticipated the answer when he asked the missionary's name.

"Robert DeKirk. Why? Do you know him?"

Tom grinned from ear to ear and chuckled, "Yeah, you could say that," going on to explain the connection.

Many of the congregation stopped to shake hands and thank them for the challenge. Mrs. Copley stayed at a table in the back of the auditorium giving out the literature Paul had created.

Brenda was among the last to come forward. She shook hands with Tom and then told him she was very excited with his spiritual growth and was so glad that God had spared his life on that cold, rainy night.

"Me too, Brenda," he said, then rolled his eyes in mock annoyance and added, "You were right again." After an exchange of grins and a hug, she moved on to speak with Paul.

Miss Benson had stayed toward the back giving space to her 'famous' son-in-law. As the crowd diminished, she came forward. "You boys did a wonderful job," she said shaking Tom's hand and telling him how proud she was. "You guys are plowing some new ground here. May God bless you in what you do for Him."

"Thanks, Mom. You know, humanly speaking you are the reason I am here. I wouldn't be doing this if you hadn't introduced me to Paul and kept after me to see it through."

"Well good. I am glad to have been some encouragement and will continue to pray for you boys."

Tom got his second hug of the night.

Paul and Brenda were still talking when Tom interrupted. "Who's up for a celebration at the ice cream parlor?" he asked. Hands went up, and the next course of action was approved unanimously.

~~~

Beep "Hi, Mr. Jenkins, my name is Barry Walters. I serve with African Christian Support Ministries. Several months ago, I spoke with Robert DeKirk, and he told me about you and your idea. Well, the church where you met him put me in contact with a woman who was able to give me your number. One of the groups we work with is in Cameroon, Africa. The recent fighting seems to be over, and we are organizing a short-term trip there with a small group to help repair damaged equipment and facilities. We also want to teach repair skills to the local people so they can help carry on the work. I am calling to see if you might be interested in being a part of that group." Walters left contact information and asked Tom to return his call.

It had been four months since the presentation at Pastor Copley's church. Tom had become accustomed to messages from Paul about another speaking opportunity, but this call was a first. He replayed the message, sure he had misunderstood, and then played it a third time writing down the name and number. He picked up the receiver and started to dial but stopped halfway through before slowly putting the phone down.

He stood there a moment, then picked up again, and dialed a more familiar number.

"Hello."

"Hi, Mom, this is Tom. Did you give my name to a Mister ... uh, a Mr. Walters, Barry Walters?"

"Yes. He told me what he was doing, and I thought you might like to talk to him. Did he call you?"

"Yeah, he left a message on my machine, but Mom, I can't do that."

"Why not?"

"I just can't, Mom. I can't teach. And Africa is halfway around the world! I've never been to Africa."

"Well, you'd never been to Wellington before you came here, and you'd never been to Oregon before you went there. The same with Vietnam. It's all still here on Earth, Tom. It's not like they're asking you to go to the moon."

"But they want me to teach. I can't teach."

"Well, what do you think you do every time you stand up in a church and explain what you and Paul are starting?"

"But Mom, teaching halfway around the world? I just can't do that!"

"Okay, let me get this straight. First, you felt you couldn't help start a missions' support organization, but when God opened the door you found out you could do it after all. Then something else comes up that you can't do, but now God has run out of power?"

All was quiet. Then finally, Alice heard, "That's not fair."

Alice laughed. "Well, you called to get my perspective didn't you? That's my perspective."

Another pause then softly, as if his mind were already traveling, "But that's so far away."

"Did you know that they have the same God in Africa that we have here in America?"

Tom caught her humor. "Yeah, I know," he said in exaggerated tones. "Why do you always have to be right? You are just like Brenda. You're two peas in a pod!"

Alice laughed. "Of course! Brenda and I have a direct line to Heaven. You really should listen to us more often." The laughter at both ends lightened the phone call. It reminded them of their silliness that night at The Laredo Bunkhouse.

"I thought they were going to kick us out," he said.

"Well, they certainly were looking at us a little strangely," she replied.

"Yeah, but it's okay now since there's nobody else to hear us."

"I won't tell if you won't tell."

"Deal," he agreed.

"Well, Tom," she concluded. "I have to meet a client early in the morning, so I better get to bed. Don't call Mr. Walters back tonight. Let's pray about it, and you can call him tomorrow. Remember, you should not stay if you are supposed to go, but at the same time, you should not go if God wants you to stay. Let's ask the Lord to give you wisdom, *again*," (she emphasized 'again') "like he has in the past and trust God to open and close doors as He wills."

"That sounds like a good plan, Mom."

"Great. Well, you get a good night's rest, Tom."

"You too."

"Okay. Good night."

"Good night. Oh, and Mom!"

"Yes?"

"Thanks. I love you."

"You're welcome, Son. I love you too. Good night."

Chapter 10 – Meeting of Hearts

The next evening Tom called Paul.

"Paul, I have a dilemma."

"What is it?"

"Well, I just got off the phone with a guy in Michigan who is organizing a two-week mission trip to Cameroon, and he wants me to be a part of the group."

"Wow," Paul replied. "My friend, the missionary."

"That's just it, Paul. I just don't know if I can do it."

"Well, the Lord won't give you a task you can't do, Tom. He will give you a task you can't do without him, but he won't give you a task you can't do with him."

"Yeah," Tom replied with some trepidation in his voice.

"Have you talked to anyone else about it?"

"Yeah, I called Mom last night and talked to Frank today. Then I called Wayne tonight just before I called the guy in Michigan."

"And what did they say?"

"They all said I should be open to whatever the Lord is doing."

"I hope you don't expect me to disagree with that."

"No. No I guess not."

After a pause, Paul asked, "How about your work at the station?"

"When Frank gets too far behind, his dad comes in to help. He really can't do a lot with his weak back, but he can pump gas and do light stuff. Frank also said he would be glad to help if you need him to work with you on the presentations while I'm gone. He was there when we spoke at Wayne's church and was at his mom's church when we shared last month, so he could give the short version I usually give."

"Well, it sounds to me like God has already been putting the pieces together."

"Yeah," Tom breathed deeply, and then with a tone of settled assurance he announced, "Okay, I guess I am supposed to go. Thanks, Paul."

"You're welcome." Paul's reply hinted there was something more he wanted to say.

"What's the matter?" Tom asked. "You don't sound sure."

"No, I am sure. I just have a dilemma of my own."

"I'll help if I can," Tom offered. There was a long pause, and then Tom heard Paul breathe a tense sigh.

"I don't know how to ask this, so I will just ask it straight out. Are you interested in Brenda?"

"Yeah, she's neat. I like her a lot. Oh, you mean as a girlfriend? No. No, she's more like the little sister I never had."

Another sigh, but this one was filled with relief. "That's good—that's uh—that's real good." There was another pause before he confided. "Tom, I am coming over there Saturday to take her to dinner. I'm going to ask her to marry me."

"I noticed that she was at several of our meetings recently and always ended up talking to you."

"Yeah, we've been dating awhile and talking on the phone. Did you know that she is the cousin of my best friend here in Wellington? Well, no, I guess you didn't know that. It was even a surprise to me."

"Well, you'll be getting a very good woman, Paul. But there are two conditions."

"What's that?"

"First, treat her like a princess; second, make sure I get the first wedding invitation."

"Done and done," came the reply.

~~~

Tom spoke with Mr. Walters on Saturday morning and gave him the decision. He wrote down dates and details. Then he told Frank when he would be gone.

A blend of nervousness and excitement, of trepidation and anticipation, would be his constant companions for the coming weeks.

~~~

Paul arrived on Saturday at 6:00 PM sharp. He rang the doorbell.

"Hi. Come in," Brenda said. "I'm almost ready; I just have to brush my hair."

In two minutes, he was walking her to his car. It was normally his business sedan, but recently he had put many extra miles on it in the pursuit of a pretty nurse who lived three and a half hours from his apartment. Tonight he hoped to begin the process of closing that gap in one direction or the other.

The restaurant was a familiar haunt to them. They liked The Ranch where they first met, but one of Paul's business clients in Johnstown had recommended The Palmer House for one of their business lunches. Since it was only a couple miles from Brenda's place and the food was good, Paul and Brenda had eaten there several times. Actually, they always enjoyed their time together anywhere, but Brenda especially liked The Palmer House.

Paul parked the car, and they got out. As they walked toward the entrance, the sun was to their backs. Paul saw that the small box he carried was visible in the shadow ahead of them, so he moved it behind his back hoping Brenda had not seen it. He requested a booth for two. When they were seated, he put the box on the seat beside him.

She ordered swordfish; he ordered the prime rib.

Laughter punctuated the conversation that evening. Talk was of life and the weather, of hopes and dreams and joys. Occasional tears moistened their eyes upon the recollections of a few sorrows. It was a special evening, as evenings like this are supposed to be.

When Brenda excused herself to the lady's room, Paul placed the wrapped gift on her side of the table. Upon her return, she paused in mid-motion as she saw it.

"And what is this, Mr. Corning?" she asked, smiling and sitting down.

He grinned and said, "Well, I'm not sure, but it looks a lot like a box." That comment earned him one of those looks that a man gets from a woman when she is pleased with an act he has committed but feels the need to make a nonverbal comment on the sarcasm that often accompanies such an act.

"May I open it?" she asked, looking up at him with a shy smile.

"Please do."

She removed the bow and unwrapped the gift, taking care not to tear the paper. When she opened the box, she saw that it contained a small, stuffed teddy bear. She smiled and looked at Paul in a way that let him know that his sarcasm was forgiven. Her smile changed, however, when she pulled the bear out of its cardboard home and found that on its left paw was a diamond ring.

She looked at Paul, mouth agape.

"Will you …. Will you marry me?" he asked.

Her face radiated happiness and between oscillating glances from Paul to the bear and then back to her friend and husband-to-be, she said, "Yes. YES. *YES!*"

~~~

Johnstown did not have a commercial airport. Tom spent the night in Wellington to catch an early flight to Michigan where he would meet up with the rest of the team. When he left for the airport, he promised Alice he would stop by to give her a complete report when he got back.

When their stay in Cameroon was almost over, Tom realized that it had included more positives than he had hoped and none of the negatives he had feared. Not that it was perfect, such trips never are, but his initial fears were unfounded, and God's grace was clearly evident.

The locals were loving and eager to learn. They marveled at Tom's skills in repairing machinery. Even what little he knew about electrical systems proved helpful. Tom *had* taught, and they had learned.

Eyes became moist at the team's departure. All, those who were leaving and those who were staying, realized they might not see many of their new friends again on this side of eternity. Their sorrow was somewhat mitigated by the confidence that they *would* see each other again on the other side! Nevertheless, even temporary sorrow is sorrow.

~~~

On the flight home, Tom reflected on God's kind provisions and made mental notes of all the exciting things that he wanted to share with Alice. He knew she would tease him about his unnecessary fears. She told him that God would prepare the way for him, but he was so elated that it just did not matter that she was right once again.

The plane landed in Wellington a few minutes after three in the afternoon. It was supposed to arrive at 2:40 PM, but the plane had encountered some unexpected headwinds. Soon, he was on the road. As he drove up to the stone house that he had come to think of as his second home, he noticed a car in the driveway. He parked out on the street, walked up onto the stone porch, and knocked on the door. To his surprise, it was not Alice who answered—it was Marsha.

The disapproval on her face was as clear as the surprise on his. She left the door open but turned, walked across the living room, and veered down the hallway. The sound that echoed from the corridor was not exactly a slam, but it was pretty close. In any event, there was no doubt that Marsha did not want him there.

When the shock began to fade, he stepped into the house, gently closing the door behind him. Alice was standing in front of the couch and looked up at him with chagrin. Tom did not know what to say. It was not his place to question what had just happened. The house belonged to Alice, and the way he saw it, her daughter had more right to be there than he did. His face conveyed his bewilderment, so Alice was first to speak. "She's getting a divorce, Tom," she said softly. That was all she said, but it was enough.

Tom was torn between wanting to share the excitement of the last two weeks and not wanting to be where he was only half welcome. "I think I should leave," he finally said.

"I'm sorry, Tom. Marsha is not in a very good mood."

"I understand. I'll tell you about the trip some other time."

"I really want to hear about it. Can I call you this evening?"

"If you're sure it won't—if you're sure it will be all right."

"Tom, I won't do anything to deliberately hurt Marsha. I still love her dearly, but I am starting to realize that she is making her own decisions and that she is going to have to accept the consequences they bring. I can't let her decisions control my life. I'll call you around 9:30 tonight."

"I'll be praying for you both, Mom."

"Thank you, Tom."

He walked out to his car, whispering the first of many prayers that would flow freely from his heart the rest of that day and into the days to come.

~~~

On his way home, Tom stopped at Darla's Diner in Parker's Lake to grab a bite before driving the rest of the way home. However, the power transformer out on the pole had shorted out and the restaurant was closed for the rest of the day. Henry J's Fast Burgers was down the street on the other side, so he decided to try them. He was tired, and he was hungry.

The clock on the wall showed a few minutes before five o'clock when Tom walked in. He was their only customer. He looked at the waitress and said, "I should have called for reservations." She laughed. He could not remember meeting her, but she looked familiar.

When he sat down, she came over to his table. "What can I get for you, sir?"

Tom scanned the menu for a moment and asked about the Henry J's Double Deluxe.

"It is a double-decker with cheese, shredded lettuce, pickles, onion, mayonnaise, and brown mustard. You get a pickle spear on the side. We can add or subtract anything you want, but that's the basic version."

"No, that sounds good just like that. Let me have one of those, uh—an order of fries—and an RC Cola."

"Comin' up," she said turning to walk to the kitchen window.

Tom sat for a moment and began to realize how very tired he was. The long return trip, the time difference, and the unexpected tension with Marsha had really worn him out. He was still facing several hours on the road; he would be exhausted when he got home.

He bowed his head to give thanks for his food. He also continued the prayer he had whispered for the last hour. Romans chapter 8 came to mind as he was confronted with the reality that he simply did not even know what to pray. "Please help them God—just help them. I don't know what to ask. Father, just help them. Please, Lord, help Alice and Marsha."

As he raised his head, he saw the young lady standing several yards away waiting for him to finish. He smiled and thanked her as she placed his food on the table.

"You're that missionary, aren't you?"

"Uh …."

"You and the other guy came to my parents' church over in West Fork when I was visiting them last month. I saw you there."

"I was wondering where I had seen you. You were on the front row over by the piano, weren't you?"

"Yeah! How did you remember that?"

"Well, I just noticed you were really listening to what we said. Are you a Christian?"

"Yes. Both of my folks became believers before I was born, and my mom led me to the Lord when I was nine."

"It's nice to see you again …" He paused and looked at her name badge. "It's nice to see you again, Lisa."

"It is nice to see you again. Uh—I'm sorry, I am not very good with names."

"Oh, Tom, Tom Jenkins." He reached out to shake her hand.

"I sure appreciate what you said that night, Mr. Jenkins."

"Please, call me Tom. My dad was Mr. Jenkins."

She smiled, "Do you mind if I sit down?"

"No, not at all. Please do." He motioned to the chair across the table.

She sat down and stared toward the table a moment before looking up at him. "What is it like to be a missionary?" she began. "What you said made me start thinking, but more about actually going overseas, rather than doing something here like you talked about. I hope that doesn't bother you."

A big smile filled his face. "I am absolutely delighted anytime anyone does what God calls them to do."

She reflected his smile with one of her own. "I will be finishing nurse's training next spring, and I was thinking about going to Africa."

While she was speaking, he took the first bite of his burger. He smiled big enough that it was hard to keep his mouth closed as he chewed. He motioned that he wanted to say something and hurriedly finished his bite, washing it down with a drink. "The reason I am smiling is that I just came back from Africa today."

"Really?" she asked. "That's fascinating! What is it like there?"

Their exchange continued for another ten minutes until two couples came in and sat in a booth on the other side of the room. Lisa excused herself.

Tom finished his meal and walked up to the cash register. Lisa was serving the meals to the two couples. She stopped and got the order from a woman and a young boy who had just come in, then waited on Tom at the register.

"Keep your eyes open, and watch for God's hand, Lisa. Remember, if you get in a hurry, you are likely to get ahead of God and that will not work out very well. He is on his own schedule. Our goal should not just be to do something for God, but rather to let him work his will through us in his time."

"But how will I know?"

"Watch, pray, and wait," he said. "Read the last four verses of Isaiah 40. Then watch, pray, and wait."

"Okay," she said, and then, as if not wanting their conversation to end she asked, "Are you in Parker's Lake often?"

"Not too often."

"Oh," she said, obviously disappointed.

"But that could change," he said with a shrug of his shoulders and a little smile. "Where do you go to church? Maybe we could set up a presentation."

"Yeah," she said. She tore the corner off a newspaper left by a lunch customer and wrote down Parker's Lake Community Church. She pointed down the street and continued, "It's just three blocks down, and the sign has the pastor's phone number on it. You could call him sometime."

"Well, actually I am going the other way. Why don't you write down your name and phone number? I can call you tomorrow, and you can give me the pastor's number."

She mentally processed his request and then repeated the smile they had been exchanging ever since he came in. "Yeah," she said. "That's a good idea."

She added her name and number and handed him the scrap of paper.

"Have a great evening, Lisa."

"You too, Tom."

As he got into his car and started the engine he thought, "I guess I could have driven a couple extra blocks, but then I wouldn't have her phone number." He played a little mental game of pretending that the whole thing 'just happened', but he knew better. It made him smile, particularly knowing that she wanted him to have her number almost as much as he wanted to have it.

He put the car in gear, took one last look through the window at his new friend, and pulled away from the curb. "Thank you Lord, for letting me meet Lisa. And Lord, she's pretty," almost as if he was telling God something that had escaped the divine notice.

~~~

The rest of the trip home was without incident but not without thought. For the next three hours, he continued to pray intensely for Alice and Marsha. Those prayers were mixed with other thoughts, other prayers, and other memories. His mind replayed the events of his life: his adoptive parents and their passing; his friendship with Glenn and his passing; Marsha and his marriage and its passing. All of it was painful. He had grieved through each phase, yet God had brought him through it all. It was only one step at a time, and some of those were baby steps, but each step had brought him to where he was today.

As he thought, it occurred to him that the reason he could have faith in God was because God himself is faithful. Tom drove, and he prayed. As the early evening unfolded, his prayers for Alice and Marsha, and now Lisa, became interlaced with worship and praise as he reflected on God's faithful love. Three hours went by very quickly.

When he arrived back home, he turned off the engine and made one last petition before he went into the house. His heart became very heavy on behalf of Marsha. He had hurt her; she had hurt him in return. Everything else and everyone else just evaporated from his mind. "Lord, you know my heart. You know that I am not asking anything for myself. But Lord, Marsha is going to be so miserable until she gets real with you. I don't even know what to ask for, except for you to move in her heart. If she is not your child, please draw her to yourself. If she does know you, please help her to understand that her life will be in constant turmoil as long as she is running from you. Please help her see that she needs to make you the center of her life. Help me to do that too, Father. Please. I pray in Jesus' precious name, Amen."

~~~

What was that noise? It was the phone. Tom jumped off the couch where he had been asleep for almost an hour.

"Hello."

"Tom?"

"Oh hi, Mom."

"Hi. I am glad you made it home safely. You looked a little tired this afternoon."

"Yeah, I was just resting when you called." He immediately wished he had not said that.

"I'm very sorry, Tom. Perhaps I should call you tomorrow night."

"No, a little nap really hit the spot. I feel pretty good now, and I really want to tell you about the trip."

"I want to hear about it too, Tom, but let me tell you something first. It's about Marsha."

"Is she okay? I've been praying for both of you."

"I think she is Tom. I really hope she will be anyway. After you left, she went out for a drive. When she got back, she had calmed down. We sat and talked awhile. It turns out she was right; I would not have approved of the guy she married. He was really using some dangerous drugs and doing all sorts of wild things. She even followed him into some of that stuff. Last month, a friend of his talked him into going to church, and Tom, he trusted in Christ! Marsha says that his life has changed completely."

"Ha!" Tom's single, excited laugh burst through the telephone line. "That is so different from what I expected God to do, but that is fantastic!" He paused and then asked, "Why is she going to divorce him?"

"Well, that's because she is not a Christian and doesn't want to change. At least, that is what she told me. She doesn't want to think about the Lord yet, but as we talked, she decided that she really does want to work it out with her husband. She called him about an hour ago, and she is heading back to South Carolina in the morning."

"That is so neat, Mom. I just never can guess what God is doing, but He is so fantastic! You remember what he says in Romans 11? 'O the depth of the riches both of the wisdom and knowledge of God! How unsearchable are his judgments, and his ways past finding out!'"

"Yes, that is for sure," she replied.

"Well, let me tell you about the trip." Tom spent the next 15 minutes giving a breakdown of the events. He got so excited that his little presentation was regularly punctuated with "Oh, and then" ... and "Oh, I almost forgot...."

As he expected, he had to endure her occasional, "I told you so!"

"I'm so glad it went well, Tom. Do you think you might go back?"

"I would really love to, Mom," he sighed, "and that brings me to another thing I want to tell you and ask you pray about."

"Okay."

"Well, I stopped in Parker's Lake for supper before I drove the rest of the way home. The waitress saw us make our missions presentation a couple of weeks ago in West Fork. We talked as much time as she could spare from her job, Mom. She wants to be a medical missionary and is thinking about Africa!"

"Reeeeally?" she said, with a smile Tom could hear through the phone.

Tom told Alice all he could remember and how there seemed to be an instant bond with his new acquaintance. His mind was reeling again. The whirlwind in his mind had stopped when exhaustion had rendered him lifeless on the couch. Now, the spinning was starting again.

"I am excited for you, Tom. Remember to go slowly and let God open the doors. I will pray for you. And if you think things are shaping up, I look forward to meeting her." Tom assured her that if the Lord opened this door, he would be elated to introduce them to each other.

When they had said all there was to say, at least as much as their exhausted minds could think to say, they made plans to speak again the next week. Each retired for the evening, remembering to pray for Wellington and Cameroon, and several points in between.

Epilogue 2

And so the story continues …. Every day, and day after day, in ways that we may never understand and for reasons best known to The Almighty alone, God reaches down into lives. Some are teetering on the edge of ruin, and He pulls them back from the abyss and claims them for his own. Others are, as John Bunyan put it, in the "Slough of Despond"—a swamp of despair. God reaches down and comforts with the tenderness of a hen brooding over her chicks. Still others are living normal, everyday lives, or so it appears. Yet, without God, even they are adrift, cut loose from their moorings, unaware of their real purpose.

God is rich in mercy. In his great love for us, God deems it best to bring glory to himself by displaying his loving kindness to those who trust in Him. He enters into our desert wilderness and plants a beautiful garden. Oh to be sure, the flowers take time to bloom, and we sometimes feel the pain of our thorns among His roses. Additionally, the garden needs tending—digging and thinning, pruning and weeding—but in the end, those nearby find the fragrance a little sweeter. The beauty has become a little more refreshing to the soul than before the garden was planted.

And what of those people in whom God plants those beautiful gardens of redemption? Well, even as imperfect as they are, God says that out of them "shall flow rivers of living water". (John 7:38)

Perhaps the old hymn says it best: "To God be the glory, Great things he hath done."

Great things God has done indeed. And still does!

Not the End

Soli Deo Gloria. Amen!

We hope you enjoyed *Streams of Mercy in the Valley of Shadows*. Please visit our web site for information about other works by the author. You will also find the author's recommended reading list.

Feel free to send us your comments too. The author enjoys hearing from his readers.

Website: www.WilliamFPowers.com

Email address: Bill@WilliamFPowers.com

Made in the USA
Columbia, SC
20 June 2017